NO

Love

LOST

BY THERONE SHELLMAN

ISBN#: 0-9771004-2-1
ISBN#: 9780977100422

Published in the U.S.A.
Third Eye Publishing, Inc.
P.O. Box 5694, Bayshore, N.Y. 11706
(516)232-0202
www.thirdeyepublishing.org
www.myspace.com/thirdeyepublishing

Cover Design/Graphics: www.mariondesigns.com

Editor: Stacey Seay

Acknowledgements:

Who I am and have become I owe to the creator first and foremost. I also would like to thank my family and friends for encouraging me to keep moving forward. To my sister Alicea, you are my heart and the only person who believed in me. Beyond words, you have always been there. To all of my girlfriends throughout the years, I would like to thank you. All of you have contributed to my learning about becoming a man. I owe you all a lot.

Since the release of my first novel, "Love Don't Live Here," I have met so many people, some for the good and others for the bad. But experience is what defines who we are, so I would take none of it back. **To everyone who bought my first title, thank you!**

The following street vendors of NYC are the ones who have been instrumental in making the title a success, Porgo, Massamba, Sidi, Nelson, and Henry.

To all the lit organizations, reviewers, bookstores, and press that I have had the opportunity to work with, I hope that we can continue our friendship. Coast2coastreaders.com (my online hang out spot), O.O.S.A online book club, Books2mention, Girlfriends, Inc. Literary and Social Organization, Delores Thornton (Around2itbooknook), Brenda and Carol (C&B Book Distribution), Alvin Romer (The Romer Review), RAWSISTAZ, The Hustlers Report News Magazine, aalbc.com, mosaicbooks.com, cushcity.com, PMA (Publishers Marketing Association), and all the African American bookstores who stocked the title, and where I've done signings. Thanks to all the African American bookstores that did not stock the title because it did not have a picture of a sexy lady with a little bit of clothing on. I would also like to thank Borders, Barnes and Noble, and the mainstream market for all the support. Also, thanks to all the online retailers who picked the title up, and because of this, I have received overseas sales.

Thank you to all the people who have reached out to me with emails. I am honored to have gotten to know all of you and be someone that you respect and admire.

Please join me and become my friend on myspace: http://myspace.com/theroneshellman, http://www.myspace.com/thirdeyepublishing

Dedication

This book I would like to dedicate to every parent who has ever lost their child to the uncaring world of the streets. I would also like to take the time to acknowledge some of my friends who are no longer here. All of them were murdered as a result of living life in the fast lane. Chikarra, Phd, Born, Chrissy, Mel, Sha, Shammel, and Shatief, who was one of my closest friends and was murdered in prison.

Let the following be a lesson to all:

At the age of seventeen, I was sentenced to four to twelve years confinement. It was throughout serving this time that I fell in love with books. I basically read everything I could get my hands on, Donald Goines, Walter Mosley, Ralph Ellison, James Baldwin, Langston Hughes, and also history books and autobiographies, which are still my favorites.

Books were my only escape from a prison world that was very harsh. Out of the four and a half years that I did, about two years or so was done in the Special Housing Unit (SHU), which is basically called the Box. This is a place you are sent as a disciplinary action after being found guilty of not following the prisons rules and regulations. Since most of my time was spent in maximum-security facilities, guys who were either doing ten plus years or never coming home surrounded me. Day in and day out, cuttings and stabbings occurred. Every day I fought for my sanity, while at the same time realizing I had to become part of the madness to survive. I found myself getting into fights and altercations both to protect myself and to establish a reputation for myself as a cat not to be screwed with. Without books, I could have never escaped the psychological abuse that I was faced with. There was one point where I honestly wondered if I was going to make it to see the day I was released. Then, another part of me wondered what I was going to make out of my life. What would I be doing when I was thirty years old? It was this torture that I unknowingly subjected myself to that ultimately drove me to seek knowledge and answers. And I found these answers and hope in books. In fact, I wrote my first manuscript eight months after being incarcerated and sent it in to a publishing house. I was told they did not accept urban fiction anymore because the public's thirst for the genre had dwindled. This was in 1989.

Remarkably, now I'm thirty-four years old, a publisher, author, visionary, and soldier. I am your brother and friend in this struggle that we all face to be the best we can be. I will always be your voice to speak out and scream out loud. I am not scared to do so, and will never be. It is my mission and purpose to educate through stories. I came from a broken home, and as a result turned to the streets at fifteen and started selling drugs. By the age of sixteen, I graduated to sticking up other drug dealers. I've seen the worst of the worst at an early age. When I came out of prison at the age of twenty-two, without any firm family and community support, I quickly found myself back into the lifestyle that I was living before as a teen. But in the back of my mind, I knew that there was something more for me. The idea to be a published writer never left. I never forgot the first manuscript I wrote. In fact, I never gave up writing. No matter what I did, I found the time to write, even if it was just five hours a week.

At the age of twenty-eight, I came home from a parole violation and finally decided that I could not live this crazy lifestyle anymore. There was not enough money in the world for me to make to give my life to the system. Which I was sure was going to happen if I kept selling drugs. It was at this point in my life that I realized that writing would save my life, so I built my every day schedule around this. I obtained my first job on the books, and set out a plan to learn and become as knowledgeable about the literature business as possible. I worked eight hours a day and I read no less than six hours a day. All the books I read about successful people told me that your passion to become successful in whatever it is has to be greater than your passion for anything else in life. My life had become literature, and at the age of thirty-three, I self-published my first novel, "Love Don't Live Here". After eight months, the book has sold a little over 7,000 copies and I've just managed to secure a national distribution deal for the title. The title was a Booking Matters Magazine Bestseller for the month of August, 2006. The same power and enthusiasm that I put into doing negativity, I now put into obtaining my dream. And this can happen with anyone when they give their all. There is a big world out there, filled with opportunities other than the negatives, which may be tempting. But the price to pay is so great that it's not worth it. I should know all about this because I started at the age of seventeen and by the age of twenty-eight, I had accumulated a total of seven and a half years in prison. Do I feel that it was worth it? Hell, no! There is nothing worth giving my life for other than family, loved ones, and a dream to help others like so many of our great leaders have given their lives for. Drug dealing, stealing, and robbing are not dreams of wealth and happiness. Instead, it is a great illusion that will provide, in the long run, a lot of pain and suffering to those involved as well as those who love them. And it hurts the community in the process.

Chapter One

"Surprise!"

The loud roar of cheers erupted once Derrik opened the front door allowing the day's bright sun-rays to beam into the living room on all the familiar faces.

Totally surprised by the group of people welcoming him home, he turned to his mother, who stood behind him. Assisting her into the house, the seventeen-year-old embraced her with such vigor she froze in his embrace. He kissed her on her plump, honey-complexioned cheeks before burying his chin in the hollow of her shoulder. He wanted to cry, and would have, if not for all the people in the room. Although he knew everyone there, his ego would not allow him to break down and reveal what the last six months of being locked up had done to him.

"I want a hug too," a voice called out.

Derrik turned from Beverly to see his sister Tinesha taking full inventory of him. She eyed him up and down, laughing in her girlish way. "Boy! Derrik you got big. You must have been lifting and eating up everything."

As he slowly let go of Beverly to hug Tinesha, she asked, "Did Supreme get out too?"

Derrik's smile disappeared as he gave her a look that said why did you have to ask that? He even glanced from the corner of his eye to see if their mother had picked up on what Tinesha asked. To his dismay, he saw that Beverly was staring in their direction. *What now?* he thought, throwing his slim, muscular arm around his younger sister, giving her the "look what you done now," look.

Staring into his eyes, Beverly screamed, "I don't want to see you with that clown anymore!"

Before Beverly could say another word, Derrik cut in, waving his right hand. "Okay! Okay! I just got home. Let's not go there." Turning toward the group of well- wishers who'd come to welcome him home, he locked eyes on his younger friend and cousin, Jermaine. Derrik forgot about Tinesha and Beverly as he stepped over to Jermaine and the welcoming crowd of fellas who surrounded him to give him daps and pats on his back. The young ladies waited their turn to kiss him on the cheek.

"Yo, what's the deal?" Derrik asked Jermaine as the two hugged one another and then shook hands in an odd looking way the fellas called dap.

"Man, I been waiting for you to get out cuz it's been mad whacked. I ain't been doing nothing. Word! Jermaine said, smiling at his mentor standing in front of him.

"Yeah, I couldn't wait to get out that dump too. Word! That was killing me." With this said, they both broke into laughter. Music started to play and the atmosphere in the room became happy as everyone began to move about the house. Some started to dance, others huddled in groups to laugh, joke, and gossip. Most of the mothers and older women walked into the kitchen.

*   *   *   *   *

"Ah, I'm glad this day is over" Beverly mentioned, looking out a living room window, seeing a car pull off from the curb out in front of her house.

Barbara yelled over her shoulder standing in front of the kitchen sink all ready at working washing dishes "Yeah, well I'm gonna help you clean up so that we can get on up outta here and go to my house after you fix dinner for the kids."

Derrik and Jermaine were sitting along the fifth and sixth steps leading to the stairway upstairs while Tinesha sat alone at the dining room table eating a large slice of the vanilla pineapple cake Beverly had bought for Derrik's welcome home party. All three came to attention once Beverly backed away from the living room window she was peeking out of and called out to them.

"Derrik, Tinesha, and Jermaine come on, Lets get this house together. Frank ain't gonna be home from the baseball game until about nine-thirty, so I'm going to Barbara's for a little while. I'll be back before he gets here." Clapping her hands strongly together she stated, "So let's go."

Placing the plastic fork she was using to eat down on the napkin in front of her, Tinesha picked up what was left of the piece of cake and started to bite at it, devouring every bit of the pastry in four bites. By the time Beverly reached the kitchen doorway, her daughter had already begun to clean up the mess of plastic ware scattered all over the table from the party.

Walking into the kitchen, Beverly heard the footsteps of the two young men coming up behind her. All ready knowing what had to be done, she turned around to tell them, "Y'all take out all these garbage bags, and then clean up the living room while we get the kitchen and dining room done. I have some rice, beans, and pork chops left over from yesterday's dinner in the fridge. Once I…"

Derrik's eyes grew big once his mother mentioned pork chops. His eyes stared from her to the refrigerator and then back to her before he cut her off. "Ma, I don't eat pork no more."

He stared at the refrigerator instead of looking at her because he knew his words were going to be met head-on and defiantly.

Everyone turned toward Derrik. Tinesha, Barbara, Beverly, and even Jermaine turned toward the muscular adolescent as if he said something so abnormal that they did not believe what they had heard and needed him to say it again.

"What?" Beverly asked, in a voice tone just under a scream. She looked at him with a penetrating stare.

Derrik did not reply quickly enough for her. So she asked again. This time placing a hand upon each hip "What did you say?"

Barbara looked toward her friend, who glanced back at her before they both looked at Tinesha, who stared at them before breaking off and looking at Derrik, but also Jermaine because the two stood only a few inches apart from one another. Jermaine's eyes, by this point, were fixed upon the shades and colors of the linoleum tiles on the kitchen floor. The last thing he wanted was to get involved in whatever mess Derrik had gotten into.

Derrik's stomach started to bubble as his nerves began to give. However, he knew he had no choice but to face the music and tell her the deal with what was on his mind. So he decided to just tell her, all she could do but get mad, he reasoned. Breaking his stare from the refrigerator and looking to her, he noticed that his mother met his stare with equal velocity and force. Yet, he did not blink or look away for one split second.

"Ma, I don't eat pork anymore."

Hissing, she went on, "Yeah, now you went to jail and became a Muslim all of the sudden. What are you gonna tell me, your name is Muhammad or Malik? Boy! It's ok with being in tune with being black. But still, what does eating pork have to do with it? You done went to jail and lost your mind!" Beverly shook her head from side to side several times, and was about to turn around and face the sink. But as she made a half turn, she decided to turn back around to the young man who had changed from the young boy she remembered, and who now stood so firm before her.

"So what do they call you now?" Beverly asked, lowering her voice a pitch or two.

"Infinite."

"Hmmm." Beverly huffed, shaking her head from left to right and once again exhaling deeply.

With a face full of sorrow and grief she stated "I went through this with your father. So what are you a Black Muslim or something?"

"No, I'm a member of Nation of Gods and Earths."

"What the hell is that?" Beverly asked, slapping the palms of both hands against her face.

The young man was about to speak, but Barbara cut him off by throwing her right hand up to her mouth, pointing, and sticking out the index into a hush, keep quiet gesture.

Beverly looked toward her friend, wearing a mask of disbelief and hurt. Barbara felt her grief and pain and grasped a hold of her friend's right hand.

"Come on, let's get out of here and go to my place. The kids can fix up here and then make whatever they want to eat. We'll be back by nine."

Looking toward Jermaine, Barbara asked her son, "Are you gonna stay, babe?"

"Yeah," he answered happily, but at the same time trying his best to conceal the fact that he did not want to be hanging with the ladies.

Beverly was still in a sense of awe and deep thought. Barbara pulled at her arm, tugging her to walk with her out of the kitchen.

"I'm coming with y'all." Tinesha blurted out, running to catch up with the quickly moving duo. Five seconds later, the front door closed leaving the two young men behind by themselves.

"I should throw all that swine in the garbage." Infinite sneered, walking over to the kitchen sink and turning on the faucet. Jermaine watched closely as Infinite began to wash the remaining dishes, handling the plates and utensils roughly and clumsily as if he was doing the last thing in the world that he wanted to do.

Just as Barbara brought the car to the end of the driveway and was about to swing the vehicle onto the street, a blue car pulled up alongside the curb next to the driveway's entrance.

"There's Tami." Tinesha stated from the back seat as she stared out the rear windshield and waved.

Bringing the car to a screeching halt, she told Tinesha, "Go tell her to follow us."

Hearing this, Tinesha more than eagerly jumped out of the car and ran over to Tami.

Beverly didn't bother to look back to see Tinesha or Tami. Neither did she look toward Barbara, whose eyes were fixed busily upon her. Instead, she stared out toward the driveway, which stretched out about 20 to 30 feet beyond the front windshield.

"Booommm," the back door slammed shut.

"Okay, let's go" Tinesha said.

Barbara removed her right foot from the brake pedal and stepped on the gas lightly, bringing the car into reverse. Then she swung a right turn onto the street before stepping on the brake pedal once again; simultaneously shifting the car into drive and pulling off. Looking into the rearview mirror, she saw the blue sedan pull off the curb and follow.

"Let's go to my place." Barbara whispered to no one in particular other than herself, as she kept her eyes pointed straight ahead on the street.

Neither Beverly nor Tinesha replied, instead, they both allowed themselves to escape into the world of their own thoughts.

"That boy's getting too grown, he's gonna have to get out my house soon, before he drives me crazy." Barbara whispered, not even realizing that she was talking out loud. The two other women looked her way; yet, each quickly decided to let the statement go without a response.

Chapter Two
Two Years Later

"Boy, what's wrong with you, all of the sudden it seems like ever since you got in twelfth grade, you've been into all types of shit. Your mother said she gives up. She's tired of your shit, and told me that if you cannot follow the rules in her house, then you're going to find your ass on the streets. That's why she asked me to speak to you. She tells me your selling drugs, or doing something because she don't be buying all them new clothes you be putting upon your black ass. And she says you always have money, and be hanging with a bunch of characters. All I'm a say is that you're headed in the wrong direction. Look at your brother, he don't get in no trouble, he does well in school. All he talks…"

Before he could say anything else, Jermaine interrupted. "First of all, I ain't my brother, and number two, you don't know me. And Ma don't know me either. You have been around a few years of my life, popping up outta nowhere. Now you think you know me! When I was a kid you weren't around, now I'm practically grown. Maybe if you were around when I was little then I'd be different and things would be different. But you weren't, so this is me."

With blood in his eyes, he stared at his father defiantly. "I'm a do what I have to do, like I been doing. So don't worry."

A loud echoing sound of two objects crashing together resounded as Trini slapped Jermaine forcefully across his right cheekbone, lifting the frail adolescent off his feet and causing him to fall to the surface of the blacktopped driveway. His body hit hard and he banged his head. His neck snapped quickly, jerking backwards upon the tarred surface. While Jermaine lay sprawled out on his back, Trini stood at his feet.

"You little fuck! Don't you ever talk to me like that again. You think you're grown? You think you're a man? You ain't nothing but a punk. You don't know your ass from your fucking feet. Now get up!"

Jermaine, holding his right hand up to his face, looked upon his father with sincere hatred pumping through his blood. And once Trini told him to get up, he jumped up on his two feet as if he never hit the black top. Defiantly, he stood before the massive man before him for what seemed to be an eternity. They stared at and into one another until Jermaine turned around and walked down the driveway, taking a right turn onto the street. All the while, he could hear his father speaking to him, but he did not bother to listen or seek to comprehend the words. Instead, he allowed the words to become a part of the day's scenery, like the chirping of the birds. He walked away and never once bothered to turn around to look back. As far as he was concerned, he was getting rid of a part of his life that never really mattered to him.

Ever since he had the argument with Trini, Jermaine found himself hanging out more and more, doing exactly what Trini didn't want him to do. Everyday now, he hung out with Derrik, who had always been a little more mature and faster than him. Jermaine had been a bit sheltered, whereas Derrik was growing up fast; especially, since he had become friends with Supreme, who was selling drugs, and into things that most teens only wished they could be a part of. Once Derrik went away to do time, he came back a totally different person. He wasn't one of the kids anymore, he was Infinite. Before this, Derrik and he were best friends; their mothers had known each other since the two boys were in grade school.

Infinite introduced Jermaine to selling weed. He and Supreme told him that if they got caught, nothing would happen because possession of marijuana was only a misdemeanor. Jermaine was scared the first few days on the block, but as the days went by, he started to build up confidence. Plus, he liked having money and being around Infinite. His friend was driving a new car, had nice jewelry, and much respect throughout the hood. Not to mention all the girls who swarmed around him like bees whenever he came through. Jermaine wanted this status as well, and at times, he was caught up between the idea finishing school and going to college to become a teacher, or being down with the street life, which seemed so enticing. The past year had been the most fun he ever had. Yeah, he argued with his mother, but this did not bother him because she was only around at night because of the long hours she worked. Jermaine hardly ever ran into his stepfather because he had a traveling job and he was in and out of the house most of the time, except on the weekends.

Jermaine knew that Infinite and Supreme were doing more than selling weed because they always had knots of money. At any given moment, they had at least fifteen hundred dollars. Selling weed was good money, but it only netted hundreds a day. One day, he got up the heart to ask them if he could get down with whatever else they were doing. Supremes' reply off the bat was for him to continue school, sell weed, and go on to college. Infinite seconded this, telling Jermaine to stack his money and save it for school. But Jermaine harassed them everyday until they finally gave in.

"Ok! We're gonna put you down!" Infinite told him with the look of regret on his face. Contemplating momentarily, he added, "We got something popping soon."

Supreme wanted to say something, but kept quiet because, he knew that Jermaine would only come back with a quick reply. He really didn't think Jermaine was built for this life, and constantly told Infinite to keep an eye on his friend and to keep him out of harm's way. Staring into Infinites eyes, the following thoughts flowed through him, *Now he's going to find out how it really goes down and I hope he don't fuck up!* He did not want to get in between their childhood friendship, but he felt Infinite was making a big mistake which could cost them all. They were going to do something big, something, which involved someone, they all knew. In fact, they copped their weed from Powerful and those cats. *I hope shortie don't freeze up on us, cuz I might have to do a whole lot of gun-clapping when this goes down,* he thought, silently rubbing his rough hands together, looking at the tips of the bottom of his fingers which were brown from smoking marijuana joints. Looking up, he saw the two talking, and decided that it was time for him to bounce.

"Yo! I'm gone. I'll get up with ya'll two gods at the power hour tomorrow.

Infinite and Jermaine yelled," Peace!" without looking his way and they continued their conversation.

***

Two Weeks Later
It was twelve-thirty AM at a rest stop on Sunrise Highway, in Long Island, N.Y., and the weather was not cold, but it was not warm either. There was a little mist in the air, so when one exhaled, smoke would come out through their nostrils or mouth.

In row, twenty-seven phone booths stood in all. This night was very quiet, except for the occasional oncoming traffic from the highway. In the parking lot, there were two trailer rigs along with two cars parked alongside phone booths. In the distance, was another car with three occupants. Everyone in the car was tense with anticipation as their eyes watched the guy at the phone booth nearest to the truck exit.

"Are we gonna get this motherfucker or what?" came from Supreme. Supreme was the one to initiate everything; at least, he felt this way anyway. Nevertheless, one thing was for sure, he was a young black male and didn't have any fear about living or dying. Which ever came the following moment, it really didn't matter to him. His life, as far as he was concerned, was nothing more than a series of disappointments. Over the last two years, he'd been to two different funerals of three good friends. He even had a fall out with his mother and moved out. Not once, had he been back to visit. As crazy as that may sound to others, life held no meaning to him anymore. "Life's a bitch and then you die," had become his favorite phrase. Whenever he was feeling down or in a gloomy mood, these were the words, which were sure to escape from his mouth.

What a mismatch of personalities the three of them were together, despite the fact that they were around the same age. Jermaine was the youngest, and unlike the other two, he was neither arrogant nor unapproachable. Yet, he was very careful whom he dealt with. His mom always told him that you never truly know who the person next to you is until its too late. Infinite had just turned twenty years old, and was similar to his mentor, Supreme, in many ways. His attitude was very hostile, but laid back at the same time. The thing that separated him from Supreme was that unlike his mentor, he was very business-like, a quality that his mom instilled in him since childhood. He was very quiet as well. As long as you did not mess with him, one would barely notice he was present. Throughout the last two years, although Infinite remained friends with Derrik, he was levels beyond his childhood friend because of his close relationship with Supreme, who had been involved in the life of crime for about seven years. Plus, both Derrik and Supreme had their own places, so they had the freedom to chill whenever they wanted.

In response to Supreme's question Infinite answered, "Yeah, gee, back the car up and let's handle this."

As the car sped into reverse, the air was filled with the sound of the car's engine, and the smell of burnt rubber emanated from the tires. When all three figures jumped out of the car with guns outstretched, the man on the phone pulled out, and without hesitation, began to shoot. The first shot grazed Supreme in his right arm, near the shoulder. The bullet burned a hole in the fabric of his jacket, leaving a hole, but luckily, not touching the skin. The nine-millimeter baby Glock the man was shooting packed a powerful punch. Every time he would bust off, the roar and fire from the barrel was so deep with melody, it sounded like a quarter stick of dynamite being lit up on the Fourth of July. Though this was so, the fact was, he was still outnumbered. Unluckily for him, a bullet struck him in the face, shattering his nose and right cheek bone, sending him convulsing and falling back towards the phone booth before laying him on his back. However, even then, it was like life wouldn't escape him, he remained semi-conscious. His body kept jerking all over until Supreme walked over to him. Standing directly with his legs outstretched on either side of the man's torso, Infinite released two nine-millimeter slugs into his upper chest.

Frantically, they searched through the victim's car, ripping through the interior like a cat pawing furniture, for what seemed to be an hour; but in fact, it was only a minute or two before Infinite came across what they were looking for, two zip-lock bags filled to the top with a powdery white substance and two envelopes full of one hundred dollar bills. "Bingo!!" infinite screamed, scooping everything up in a hug-like motion.

Running in step, like in a military drill, all three assailants jumped into the car. Once inside, each looked at one another, deeply staring into each other's eyes, but not saying one word. The engine cranked, there was no need to explain what had just taken place back there. It was better him biting the dust than any one of them-and this was a reality, which resonated in all of their minds at this very moment.

Jermaine sat speechless, too scared to even blink or tremble for that matter. As they were pulling away he could see the truckers getting out of their trucks to take a look at the remnants of what happened. It's a good thing it was misty outside because it made it almost positive that no one could decipher the cars license plates.

Smelling and sensing Jermaine's fear Infinite asked, "Gee, you all right?"

Jermaine was shaken up, but he didn't want to sound like a punk. The last thing he wanted was for Infinite to think that he did not approve of what Supreme did concerning the situation— something he did not want to think about ever again, *the murder*. For all Jermaine knew, he could be the next one to get it if he didn't play it right. Supreme was a loose cannon for sure, and there was no question in Jermaine's mind before this happened that he was capable of murder. This situation just confirmed it. Thinking this through he replied, "Yeah, it's all good over here." As he said it, he couldn't look Infinite in the face though.

Looking at Supreme, Infinite winked before turning over to Jermaine stating, "Yo, from now on, kid, every one's gonna call you Blaze because you handled that steel tonight like a welder handles a torch. Word to life."

Feeling a little nauseous as his stomach muscles pinched together violently, Blaze asked, "Do you think any one's gonna find out that we followed Powerful back from Queens?"

"Nah," Supreme chimed in. "Plus them clowns think they're so organized that no one is smart enough to infiltrate them like we did. So don't sweat it. As matter of fact, fuck them lames! Count the doe."

Blaze's hands shook, but without hesitation he began to count. The night to him was like a dream and a nightmare put together in one. Never in his life had he ever shot anyone. Yet it didn't seem like such a big deal. It was just the necessary thing to do given the circumstances. At least, that's what it seemed like to everyone else he knew who shot someone. Plus, fellas in the hood were getting shot all the time. But he did shiver at the thought that maybe it was his bullet that sent Powerful back to the essence.

As Blaze counted the bills he thought, "Well, that's life. You win some and you lose some." His nerves were starting to balance out a bit as he continued to count. Never in his life had he counted, or even seen, for that matter, so much money. This shit was real though and he could feel it. The money felt like brittle loose-leaf paper. He could smell it, the sheets smelled like glue. And the best part about it was that he possessed it. The reality of the money in his hands brought a sense of greed and reality to a situation that was totally inhumane by the principles that his mother had tried to instill in him. The danger excited him.

While Blaze counted, Infinite and Supreme said nothing, and made no movement except when Infinite placed a tape in the cassette deck. The sound of the one of the neighborhood DJ's music could be heard blasting from the speakers and tweeters. As the tones blasted, Infinite rocked back and fourth, driving on and contemplating about the days when he was a kid and used to be happy just seeing his mother wear a smile. Money didn't matter, females didn't matter, and he didn't have constant thoughts about survival or death.

Motioning for Infinite to turn the radio down, Blaze screamed, "There's eleven thousand, two hundred."

Smiling, but looking straight ahead at the street in front of them Infinite stated, "Split it up. Three ways, OK."

It was more than OK for Blaze. But at the moment, all he could say was, "Yeah, all right. Yo, what about the coke? What are we gonna do with it?"

With a smirk on his face, Supreme laughed, stating, "Yo, gee, we're about to get on for real! We're gonna make this happen. Fuck all these lames doing their thang, we're gonna blow for real!"

Blaze liked the sound of this so much that he became tongue tied for a moment before deciding not to say anything. Instead, he just laid his head back and began to doze off to sleep.

"What's up?" Blaze said, about ten minutes later, waking out of his sleep and rubbing both eyelids.

"We're at your house, sun." Infinite said.

Realizing what this meant, Blaze awoke fully. "Y'all hold the coke and we'll get up tomorrow. I can't take this shit inside the house cuz I don't have any place to hide it. Plus, you know my mom is mad nosey. She'll know that I'm up to something if she sees me carrying a bag. Plus, ever since you moved out the house, your moms and my moms be saying that you lost your mind and that I should stay away from you before I end up in jail or dead."

Listening to Supreme's snoring, Infinite contemplated for a moment and smirked, quickly turning his face into a frown "Don't sweat it gee, tap me on my pager tomorrow at one o'clock. Then we'll get up."

Giving Infinite a pound, Blaze bounced up outta the car bopping all the way to his front door. It was four in the morning, so he realized everyone should be sound asleep, unless it was one of those occasions when his mother would awaken after hearing him place the key in the front door. Fortunately, this was one of the times that all was well and everyone was sound asleep.

Once inside, Blaze tiptoed through the hallway, striving to hold his trembling down to a minimum. Opening the door separating the upstairs from the main floor really slowly so that it would not make a creaking sound, he crept in the hallway. Once upstairs and inside the safety and comfort of his room, the first thing Blaze did was close the door behind him. Taking the envelope from his pocket, he took out a thousand dollars before lifting up a corner of the dresser putting the envelope under it and placing it back down carefully, so as to not awake anyone downstairs. Once he was done, Blaze placed the thousand dollars among the junk in his top dresser drawer and jumped in the bed without getting undressed. Lying on his back fully clothed, he broke out into a clammy sweat from head to toe, making him feel cold and hot at the same time. By this time, it was all ready four forty-five in the morning and he knew he had to be up in a few hours. So he closed his eyes, and miraculously, was able to block out the night's events and enter a deep rest.

Usually, Blaze dreamt pleasantly. But tonight was a night that surrounded him with emptiness, questions, fear, and a level of excitement that caused him to have a restless sleep. *Man, my moms can never find out about this*, were the last thoughts that came to him as he dozed off.

Chapter Three

I f one stood outside the yard of one of the houses, which existed off exit 56 on Sunrise Highway, they could see flashing lights in the distance. These lights were coming from the ambulances and crime scene police units on the scene at the truck stop on the shoulder of the highway about a quarter mile before the exit.

"Detain any possible witnesses for questioning and close off this immediate area right now. And I mean like yesterday!" Everyone understood this as an order and without hesitation got to work. The orders came from the voice of Ronald Aldoe, the sergeant of detectives in the third precinct. To everyone on the force, he was known as Ronald McDonald. Of course, this was said safely behind his back. The detective was the type of guy who no matter how serious or mad he was, he still looked like he wore a smirk. The fact that he had red hair, freckles, and a young-looking face, although he was thirty-seven, didn't help any. But nevertheless, the man knew his job well and was an excellent cop all around, in the streets and out, not to mention that he was a ten-year vet on the force. And only two of those years were spent as a blue and white.

"This is gonna be one of them nights." Detective Aldoe thought to himself while he puffed on a cigar, filling the air with the stale smell. As the crime scene unit worked vigorously to seal off the area and make the necessary preparations for the investigative team to do their job, news reporters were everywhere, asking questions and bothering anyone they could get a bit of information from so they could formulate a story.

Detective Aldoe was trying to decipher the situation for himself, whispering "What the fuck happened here? We have one black man dead at a truck stop of all places. What the hell was he doing at a truck stop?"

Shaking his head as if in disbelief or deep thought, he paced back and fourth, oblivious to all the happenings around him. Suddenly, he was awakened out of his thoughts by a familiar face, a news reporter by the name of Carla Simmons. Ms. Simmons, as he called her, was an old friend of his. More like an old fling by anyone else's standards. She was about five foot six, weighed about one hundred-fifteen pounds, and had a complexion, year around, of someone who frequented the beach or a tan parlor regularly. Mentally she was on point, sexually she was a maniac. This is what detective Aldoe liked about her most, the fact that she sexed him like one of those porno stars. The thought of this gave him an instant bulge in his groin. Trying to conceal his perverted thoughts, he strived to look bewildered, as if the happenings of the night's situation had him utterly confused. The truth was, he'd seen plenty of young black men lying dead with bullet holes throughout his ten-year career.

Ms. Simmons was fully aware of the power she had over Detective Aldoe's psyche, so as she approached, she formed her sexiest smile for him before saying, "Detective, what do you think about this situation that exists here? Are there any witnesses who can account for what took place? Was the victim a truck driver? Do you think there was more than one person involved in this murder?"

Before she could keep asking questions, Detective Aldoecut her short, "Listen, Ms. Simmons, as soon as we the authorities find out exactly what took place, you the media and the public will know. For now, all we have is that there is one man slain."

He stopped to let his comment settle in for a moment before continuing, "At the moment, we don't have any witnesses to account for what happened. But you never know what the future holds for us, Ms. Simmons."

With that said, he turned around, stepping into the sealed area where police officers stood guard, blockading it from onlookers and press people. Once behind the blockade, Detective Aldoe turned around to wink at Ms. Simmons. To this, she just looked with a scowl on her face and turned on her heels, shaking her bottom seductively as she walked toward the vehicle. For a minute, he swore she called him an asshole under her breath as he winked at her. But he discarded the thought quickly after thinking about what type of person she was mentally. Rather than resort to such childish tactics, she'd rather get him back in her own way. He wasn't concerned because she had all ready done all she could do to hurt him when she broke off their relationship abruptly. It was then he realized she, to cunningly obtain whatever information she needed to concoct her stories, administered the sexual favors.

One of the detectives approached him, bringing him back to reality. "Hey! We have two possible witnesses who were present at the time of the shooting, but neither can identify any suspects. Both state that there was more than one individual involved in this casualty. Apparently, there was a shoot out between this guy and at least two assailants. Due to the mist in the air, neither of them could clarify exactly what happened." After he shared the new information, Detective Jackson, one of the two only black detectives on the force, stopped abruptly to let his superior think it out.

Taking the cigar out his mouth with his right hand and scratching his head with the left, Detective Aldoe stated coolly, "I guess we'll just have to wait for the forensics team to decipher how many guns were used tonight. For now, partner, let's get out of here and get to our families so we can get some sleep."

Looking at his watch, he stated, "Damn!" throwing the cigar to the awaiting street and darkness before continuing. "It's six o'clock in the morning; let the crime scene handle the rest of this shit. We'll pick up the pieces tomorrow."

With the order stated, Detective Jackson walked off. And in the distance, as Detective Aldoe walked to his car, he could see detective Jackson speaking to officers in the crime scene unit, making sure every detail would be taken care of to the tee. This was what he liked about the younger detective; the guy was thorough, which made his job that much easier. With this in mind, he revved up the Lincoln, placing the gear into drive and speeding, striving to beat time so that he could catch his wife cooking breakfast and preparing the kids for school.

*   *   *   *   *

Blaze awoke at nine o'clock the next morning. Usually at this time, he'd be in school, but he decided the night before to take the day off and go shopping for some gear. His mother was already off to work, which was a routine she followed every morning so she could take the forty five minute drive to downtown Manhattan and be at work by 8 o'clock. Since she was gone already, he didn't have to worry about the drama she would have put him through for not being at school. With this in mind, he was definitely relieved.

Just as he was about to jump in the shower, the phone rang. For a minute, he forgot no one was home and he started to dress, but then remembered and ran to the kitchen, naked. Picking up the phone receiver he asked "Who is it?" The sweet voice of Deana, one of his shorties, came through, causing him to blush. "Why ain't you in school? I was wondering where the hell you were when I didn't see you in first period."

After pausing she stated, "I miss you," in the cutest voice she could make.

"I miss you too, but I have to take care of something, so I'll see you tomorrow. I'll give you a call at your house after school, okay." He paused before saying "So maybe we can get up later." He knew she would love to see him, which was the reason why he added the comment.

In reply she stated, "You better call me at two-thirty sharp...I love you."

It was about 11 o'clock in the morning when Blaze caught the train at Babylon, Long Island to Penn Station, N.Y.; the ride took one hour and a half in all. Then, from there, he switched to the "A" train (express) to uptown Manhattan. Getting off at 125th Street in Harlem was like entering another world, black faces were all over the place, brothers and sisters were everywhere; so were black-owned businesses. One could tell by the soulful music that was blasting, that this was black people's territory. Blaze didn't know where to begin, so he decided to bounce up the strip and shop as he strolled along store to store. He knew he had to get back around the way because there was business to take care of. Plus, he had to call Infinite in a minute or so; therefore, there was no time to waste in searching for a pair of kicks (sneakers). Walking out of footlocker with a pair of Uptowns, he saw a phone booth and decided he'd call Infinite. After dialing the number three times, he finally realized he had to dial the number "one" before dialing the area code and then the number. After getting it right, the call went through, and on the third ring, Infinite picked up. "Yo, what's the deal?" Blaze asked.

Answering as if he just awoke, Infinite asked, "Peace God, what's going on? Word, I just awoke up. Where you at?"

Blaze replied, "I'm uptown on, one-two-fifth. I gotta get some gear, you need something, gee?" For a minute Infinite was quiet but then replied "Yeah, sun, get me some white Uptowns with the green Nike sign, size 10 ½. And god, try to get back by five o'clock cuz we gotta get with some cats to put something together, and get that coke off."

Chapter Four

In a house situated on one of the back streets in Flushing Queens, N.Y., nine figures were in a furnished basement, seated at a long rectangular-shaped table. Most of the individuals specialized in the art of taking money. Some of them also partook in selling narcotics, preferably crack/cocaine, which was also known in the hood as base.

The meeting was set up so that all the individuals could come to some type of agreement and to establish an understanding so each of their operations could run more smoothly. Recognizing that there is strength in unity, they knew that the more minds involved, the more opportunities there would be to make money, which was the goal at hand.

The meeting did not start until everyone was present; this did not happen until about 10PM when Hassan and Rassan arrived. To everyone on the streets they were known as Knowledge (Hassan) and Knowledge-Knowledge (Rassan) because they always watched, listened, and observed, and very rarely would speak unless it was necessary. Alike in so many ways, it was no wonder they were biological twins. They were an army unto themselves.

Now the others in the group were Kariem, Takim, Freedom, Jasheem and Divine. They were known as MPR, which stood for Money-Power-Respect. Their main access to bread and butter on the streets was through selling cocaine, yet occasionally, they would do a sting (robbery) if the price and opportunity were right.

The third group was made up of Infinite (Jermaine) and Blaze (Derrik). The two were invited because Infinite met Knowledge while he was serving time a few yrs back.

The meeting opened up with Takim speaking first. Just by his stance and the air about him, one could tell he was very respected and knowledgeable concerning his profession and the daily dealings of ghetto politics. He opened up stating, "I would like to say peace to all the brothers here." After pausing for a second he added, "I say peace because, peace is the absence of all confusion. So it is my hope that by the end of our meeting we come to some type of mutual agreement and understanding. Right now, I speak on the behalf of MPR, but by the end of this meeting, I hope to see and feel that all born out of the nine of us are one unit—family. So let's begin fellas."

"First of all, this is what MPR brings to the table. We can provide access to channel money and make more money, which is the object of the game. Our main business is selling narcotics, while your main business is taking money and drugs. Through us, you can take your money and make more money. Secondly, we can get off for you the product that you come across for a reasonable price. We'll pay twenty dollars for every gram, and for every ten thousand we receive, we're willing to give fifteen thousand at the end of a thirty-day period. Plus, we have knowledge and insight into our competition's whereabouts, which means more money for you fellas. Either way you look at it, it's just a good situation for all of us to join forces." Not saying anything else, Takim crossed his hands in front of him and looked around the room once. Everyone was contemplating about Takim's words, and what they meant for them all. They were all in deep thought for a few minutes before Infinite decided to speak "I don't think anyone here can argue that it would be good for us all to get together. It may sound stupid, but I do not really trust anyone beside Blaze. How do I know, being younger than all of you, that I can trust y'all to respect us and do business honestly with us?"

Once again, it took everyone a little while to contemplate. This time, Rassan spoke. "Trust is the basis to any relationship and a man's word is his bond. And his bond is his life. And if a man's word should falter, than there is no bond, or respect for his own life. So therefore, his life should be taken. Basically, what I'm saying is that the agreement that we make here today, everyone here is held accountable for. Our lives are as one, and if anyone disrespects this, then they shall be disrespected and lay in a pine box for eternity. Word is bond!"

Considering the reputation that he and his brother had, you could tell by the look on everyone's faces that no one doubted that he meant what he said. So to this, all nine heads could be seen nodding up and down in agreement before everyone stated "Peace!" There was nothing else to say, the bond was sealed, so they all shook hands at the same time embracing one another. The Brotherhood Family was established.

*   *   *   *   *

Every morning Blaze would go down to the neighborhood park and do pull-ups, push–ups, and crunches before running ten laps or so around the park perimeter.

On this day, as he finished his routine and was about to run, an ill feeling came over him. For some reason, an image of Supreme and his mother came to him. He remembered how Supreme had decided the day after the shooting that he was going to change his life and enlist into the army. Supreme had he cried and begged God to forgive him for what happened that night. But he swore that he would always keep the secret between the three of them and God. After that day, neither Blaze nor Infinite saw or heard from him again. Supreme was probably the coldest cat that he had seen growing up, so it was kind of weird that all the sudden he wanted to change. Maybe he had a hell of a nightmare that night. The memory of that night's events made Blaze think about his mother and how she worked so hard and sacrificed so much to give him a good life and steer him in the right direction. He felt remorse for the life he emotionally felt drawn to, but at the same time, his mom just didn't know what was truly in his heart. He felt alive and comforted by his friends in the streets. They were his home away from home. The streets were like the father he always wanted to get to know. The streets, he believed, would show you love if you show them love.

Right now he missed Supreme, and it was weird to think about it. High school was over; the streets were his new education. As a youngster and outsider to the game, he always looked up to, Infinite and Supreme, even though they were only a few years older than he. Supreme always showed him love and treated him like a younger brother. As a matter of fact, Supreme and Infinite were the ones who introduced him to the game, or life of crime. Now to most people, this may seem like a bad thing. And when his moms found out the extent of it—she was gonna have a heart attack for sure. But the reality to him was that this life was more accessible to him than becoming a professional athlete, lawyer or politician. How many people could make more money than the average professional with just a high school diploma? Crime provided an easy route out of poverty and the slums, almost over night. This can be seen through passing through any ghetto. How else could a teenager afford a thirty or forty thousand-dollar vehicle, wear gold and diamonds around their neck, fingers, and wrists? Or make thousands of dollars a day?

As Blaze jogged the quarter mile home on this Saturday morning, the offices of the third and fifth precincts were busy. The narcotics and homicide squads of both departments were putting together a joint task force unit. The word was out from a snitch on the street, who happened to also be a drug dealer; that a syndicate of both robbers and drug dealers existed and was working in unison within the county of Suffolk. He claimed that they went under the name of the Brotherhood, and that there were about fifty members in all. He also claimed that one of the leader's names was Infinite. According to the informant, Infinite had supposedly robbed him at gunpoint at his home the night before.

***

It was about seven o'clock at night on a Friday. Usually, any Friday would be a good day because it spelled the end of the week. But for Infinite, today was not his day at all. It all started with an argument he had with this clown they called Boom at the flea market in Nassau County. Infinite and his cousin King were looking for a parking space, and just as they were about to pull up into one, another car, a Mercedes utility truck, cut them off and damn near crashed into the front of Infinite's infinity. As soon as this happened, Infinite slammed on the brakes almost sending King through the windshield and causing him to slam his right knee into the dashboard. Cursing he shouted "What the fuck is wrong with you asshole?"

At that moment, Infinite jumped out, amped, walking toward the truck with a Glock at his waist. Before he could even approach the vehicle, two figures jumped out, one from each side. Both were young, in their early twenties or so, and dressed in the newest urban wear, donning chunked pieces of diamond out jewelry. Anyone could tell just by the looks of them that they were getting the riches. Once Infinite approached the truck, the guy who jumped out on the driver's side said "My bad, partner." It wasn't what he said, but the way he said it that sent Infinite to the boiling point. The man had said it as if it was no big deal that he almost swiped his car.

Infinite was enraged. "N-gga, you know you almost took the front of my car off. What the f-ck is wrong with you? You seen me getting ready to park there!" before he could say anything else homeboy cut him off, pointing his finger at him as if he was poking something, yelling back "Broke ass n-gga, who the fuck do you think your talking to? You act like your really driving something, that there is pocket change for me kid." Just as the man was about to say something else, Infinite pulled out his Glock. But at the same time he did that, a guy got out the truck's passenger side and pulled out. It seemed like perfect timing because as Infinite pointed the gun at Boom's forehead, Boom's partner had his piece leveled on Kings' chest.

Damn, he thought to himself "It's too bad King didn't carry anything."

Laughing and revealing his gold-capped teeth, homeboy told Infinite, "Yo, sun, you're good, but not today. I heard about you cats. We'll see each other again, just remember my name is Boom." With this stated, he opened up the driver's door, never turning his back toward Infinite as he got behind the wheel and backed up the vehicle. Then his partner got in as he kept his gun pointed in the direction of Infinite, who still had his Glock pointed as well. This remained so until they were out of each other's eyesight.

Slamming the Glock back into his pant's waistline, Infinite turned to King exclaiming, "I'm a get that p-ssy! We're gonna find out where his heart is really at! I don't give a f-ck who he is or how much money he's getting. That ass is mine, and that's for real." Turning fully to King he asked, "Ain't that, that kid from Wyandanch that everyone be talking about?"

Before King could reply to this Infinite added, "Doesn't he live off of Arlington off of Straight Path out there?"

King did not know the cat up close and personal. But he did see him out the way on several occasions because; King lived in Amityville, which is the next town over. So he replied, "Yeah, I be seeing him out in Wyandanch but I don't know where the cat rests at. But we can call Savior and find out cuz he had drama with them cats like two months ago."

As if a light bulb flashed inside of Infinite's head, he started to smile then said, "Word, let me call the god and see what's the deal with that cat. I wanna see where his head is at cuz right now I feel like reaching out and touching him something serious. Know what I mean?"

Getting back in the car, Infinite picked up the cell phone and threw the car into reverse as he asked King "Now I'm not even in the mood to go shopping. What's the god's number?"

King replied "286-4302."

Dialing the number, Infinite punched the car into drive, listening as the phone kept ringing on the other end.

"Peace! Who is this?" Savior asked.

"Yo, god, this is Infinite. I had to get in contact with you cuz, you know that cat Boom that y'all had drama with in the Danch?"

To this Savior said "Yeah—that big head cat who swear he the king of NY."

Infinite continued. "Today I was at the flea market and I was about to go into a parking space, and this clown cuts me off for it. So anyway, we got into some words and I pulled out, but some kid he was with pulled out at the same time. My piece was pointed at Boom, and his homeboy's was pointed at me. Word god, but to make a long story short, I want to get at that kid for real."

Savior, who was now amped up, stated, "Inf, that coward stays right on Arlington off of Straight Path with his girl. Word is bond; that guy is a coward but I know he's holding. He has to be sitting on some cheddar. He's an easy victim sun, half the time he's not home but his girl comes home from work at four and then leaves to go to night school. Then she comes back at around ten. Believe me, I thought about jacking the lame myself, but he knows my whole government name. So that's why I left it alone. He's accessible though, real easy."

Listening to the lay out, Infinite decided that he heard all that he needed to hear. "God, good looking, I'm a look into it, word."

They both said "Peace!" and hung up.

As Infinite approached the red light, he decided to call Blaze. But not until he first dropped King off because even though King was his little cousin, Infinite didn't trust him when it came down to sticky affairs. That's how it was with Infinite; he didn't trust anyone who did not live by the gun. Plus, King was the innocent type; all his life he'd been spoon-fed and didn't know what it was like to be hungry or deprived of just the basic necessities of life, like love from both parents (father and mother). So how could Infinite trust his freedom and life with someone who never had to fend for their own?

After dropping King home, Infinite, with a mischievous grin on his face, tapped Blaze on his pager. Two to three minutes later,

Infinite's cell phone was going off "Yo Blaze, what's the deal?" Infinite asked.

"Nothing lord, what'cha doing?" Blaze asked.

"I got us a victim, some big willy cat from Wyndanch. I got into some words with him earlier at the flea market and I pulled out. At the same time, his man backs out on me. I'm glad I was with King instead of you cuz we would have probably had a show down in broad daylight, word. Yo, the coward's holding some doe (has a lot of money). Plus, I know where he lays his head at with his wisdom (woman). It's a done deal, god; that cat's had."

Before he could say anything else Blaze cut him short, "Word, gee I need some recreation anyway. As a matter of fact, sun, let's get that coward A.S.A.P." With that stated they both said, "Peace," and hung up.

*   *   *   *   *

As soon as the sun goes down in Wyandanch, the back streets become damn near pitch black due to the poorly lit, and in some areas, unavailable, streetlights along the blocks. Crack heads and winos roamed the streets like zombies, appearing and walking into and out of paths behind houses and out of woods.

Boom's residence was the nicest house on the block, but had it not been for all the renovation done to it, it would have been just as ordinary as the rest of the houses in the dreary neighborhood. Instead, it stood out in the night's ever-present darkness. Around the perimeter of the house stood five-foot shrubs outlined by a four-foot fence. The color of the house was a bright yellow, which caused the scenery to look peaceful, even at night. Yet this night was to be different than all other nights.

It was about 9:45 PM when three men positioned themselves, hiding. They were all wearing black from head to toe, and armed heavily. Neither was an amateur, so all knew what was about to take place and the ins and outs of a situation that could turn out to be very hostile.

At about 10:10 headlights could be seen in the distance approaching steadily. As the car reached the driveway of 118 Arlington Avenue, the doors of the two-car garage began to lift upwards, receiving the vehicle. When the Mercedes reached the garage, three figures crept behind closely as the doors closed all four occupants within. Once inside, the driver stepped out of the vehicle wearing a navy blue business suit and high-heeled pumps, sporting a decent-sized herringbone around the neckline, and a diamond bracelet around her right wrist and what could be seen as an expensive watch on the left. She was extremely beautiful, her complexion was similar to the color of caramel, and her hair was jet black and fell to both shoulders. Just taking one look at her, all three assailants had the same thought in mind, and that was that she was just too beautiful to hurt. Yet, they'd do it if necessary. This they all knew, it was defiantly nothing personal but she was just a victim of circumstance, a casualty of war.

Moving from their positions from behind the car all of them surrounded her with Glock outstretched. Infinite was the only one to talk "Don't scream, if you do then we'll kill you. The only chance you have to live is if you cooperate. We don't want you, we want what your boyfriend has, so let's take a walk inside."

She couldn't hide the fact that she was a shaken up a bit. Beads of sweat formed on her forehead as she walked with the three gun-toting men inside the house. Her face was pale and without emotion; she looked as if she seen a ghost. All that was on her mind was that the privacy of her home had been invaded.

After entering Boom's house, Infinite sat her down on the couch, duct taping her mouth, arms, and legs heavily. She gave no fight, realizing that she had no wins. While he was taping her up, the other two searched every cubic inch of the house, starting with the finished basement where there were three rooms. One of the rooms was Boom's personal lab. Blaze was the one who came across this room. After moving one of the file cabinets situated in the corner, he noticed that one of the tiles on the floor was sticking up a little. Picking up the tile, he found that it was held by two latches on one side, which enabled it to swing up and down from the floor like a door on its hinges. Opening it would enable one to see the top part of a safe exhibiting the dial to unlock the combination. Blaze knew there was no use trying to open it himself because he didn't know the combination, so he decided to keep searching. The safe would have to wait.

After searching all the rooms in the basement, they started looking around upstairs, which took about another hour. By this time, it was 12:15 in the morning. Infinite, Blaze, and Freedom stood in the kitchen huddled in a circle talking in whispers. Basically, they were discussing whether or not they should mess with the safe, and how they were going go about getting Boom's girlfriend to tell them the combination, assuming she even knew it all. They discussed whether the safe was really worth it. They already had in their possession 1200 grams of cocaine, eighteen thousand in cash, and a small black suede-velvet bag containing jewelry.

Just as all three of them came to the decision that they were going to bounce with what they found, headlights from a car could be seen coming into the driveway. Fully alert and on point, all three grabbed a hold of their artillery, stomped out the doorway, and down the driveway.

Boom was not even aware of what was happening, and by the time he did, all he really saw were three dark figures running with guns and knapsacks in their hands. As they ran past him, one figure raised his signature of death, stating, "Yeah, we see each other again, you punk bitch!" before pistol-whipping him into unconsciousness.

Chapter Five

The scene is always jumping at a housing complex called Hempstead Terraces. The scenery is still Long Island, yet this area is not as rural as the rest of the suburb. Delis and little bodegas remained open into the early mornings. Everyone from drug dealers and hookers, to just young people hanging out, could be seen walking up and down, and around the strip.

On some nights, the detectives would try to enforce curfews, seeking to clear the streets. But still business would go on, just in a different manner than usual. There were many dealers in the area, but for the most part, the terrace was MPR territory. Kariem, Takim, Freedom, Jasheem, and Divine were the ghetto superstars in this hood. The females loved them, and the guys envied and hated them.

Most of MPR's workers were young kids ranging from the ages of 14 to 17, and they were wild uncontrollable and unpredictable. These kids were both hated and feared by all the addicts who frequented their drug spots. It was not unusual for you to walk down the block and see them beating down a crack head, or unleashing their pit bulls on someone who was acting a little rowdy or feisty and would not stay in line. This was the line, which was made by all the addicts waiting their turn to cop a product.

Everyday was an episode, but today happened to be one unto itself. There were three shifts that worked in each spot; 8 AM to 4 PM, 4 PM to 12 AM and 12 AM to 8 AM. The shift that worked from 4 PM to 12 AM consisted of Little Daz, Shawn, Ray-Ray, Mike, and

Jah-Jah. Every day after work they would all meet up and hang out. Occasionally, they'd all go out, but usually they'd stay around the way getting into all types of things to pass and occupy their time.

Tonight was unlike most Friday nights, because of the quietness that loomed around the surrounding streets like a plague. The five youths noticed this as they made their usual trip down the strip towards the 24-hour bodega. All along the way, they made noise harassing the hookers and junkies they passed by. One crack head named Heather, who frequented their spot regularly, noticed them and called out to Ray-Ray, who served her on a regular basis "Hey, shortie Ray-Ray, come here."

Ray-Ray was the arrogant pretty boy type, so to make himself look good he replied, not breaking step with the others "I'll catch you on the rebound. We're going to the 24 hour store."

Not saying anything else to him, Heather just watched the five of them walking in the distance.

Heather had to be about twenty-three yrs old. You could tell she had to have been a knock-out before she started messing with crack. Don't get it wrong, she was still a looker, but a lot of the beauty and glamour that she once possessed had disappeared. She was the type of girl that all the guys lusted after back in the day, but very few could get. Now, she was available to anyone who could and would supply her addiction. The situation was so bad that she would do almost anything to get a hit. Guys who used to lust after her now laughed at her in and out of her presence. They took enjoyment in having her perform sexual favors. In their eyes, she was no longer worthy of being treated like a prize.

Walking into the store, Jah-Jah noticed that Maria was working behind the counter, so he tapped Mike on the shoulder, "Yo, sun she's working tonight." Maria was the daughter of the storeowner everyone called him Papi. The majority of the people who frequented the place hated him because he did not conceal his out right disdain for blacks, even though the store was situated in a predominately black populated neighborhood. He'd watch everyone who came inside the store with his beady eyes like their main objective of coming into the store was to steal something.

He kept a close eye on all the young black guys who came in because of his daughter, who was obviously attracted to them. God forbid if she ever brought one of them home. In his view, all those guys were good for is making babies, abusing women, and getting locked up. Papi could not let those things happen to his dear Maria, she was just seventeen years old.

Maria caught glimpse of the five youths right away as they walked in, but there was only one she specifically looked for. The special guy was Jah-Jah, who winked at her to let her know that she was on his mind as well. He dared not speak to her though, with her father around--hovering over her every move like a vulture on a carcass. Most of the time they'd see one another her father was somewhere in sight. There was only one time that they even exchanged words. This happened when a delivery was being made by Coca Cola to the store, so Papi was too busy conducting business to watch over her every move.

All five of the youths knew that pops was eyeing them like a policeman on duty, so they walked around the store playfully, as if lost. Maria laughed, because she knew exactly why they were doing what they were doing. Usually they would do this for about ten minutes or so. But there were other things to do that night. Therefore, they decided they'd give the old man a break. After getting all they needed and placing everything on the counter, Jah-Jah decided that he would pay. The fellas obliged. Plus, they knew he wanted to play big willy in front of Maria. Pulling out a knot of twenties and tens he took out a ten and handed it to her, touching her hand gently. She smiled, touching his hand longer than necessary as well, when she gave him back change. This was the little game they played with one another everyday.

Strolling out of the store last, Jah-Jah caught up with the fellas stating to all four but to no one in particular, "Yo, sun, I'm a get that one day. The hell with Papi, he can't hold on to her forever."

"You know how them Spanish cats are sun, they don't want no Negroes messing with their ladies. You're gonna make that old man assassinate your ass. Don't let me find out one day that, that old man beat your ass, word." Mike chuckled, causing everyone else to laugh, even Jah-Jah.

But he still stated, "Screw Papi, I'm a make his daughter my mami." All five of them started laughing once again as they proceeded down the strip.

As they reached the block, an idea came to Little Daz, who was the craziest out of all of them. Laughing to himself he said in a half whisper to no one in particular yet loud enough for Ray-Ray to hear, "Let's get that bitch to suck our dicks."

At the moment, all motion stopped and they stood as if in a stupor, looking at him. They didn't know whom he was talking about. For a minute, Jah-Jah was gonna say something, but then he decided not to because he just knew that Little Daz could not be talking about Maria. Everyone wondered what he was talking about without speaking. Eventually, Ray-Ray asked, "Get who to suck our dicks?"

"That crack head freak, Heather." Little Daz stated smiling, seeking to gain their approval. It took a minute for the majority to agree, the only one who didn't was Jah-Jah, who was like this sometimes, but in the end, he usually agreed. This he noticed himself, so it's a wonder he would resist temptation in the first place. And this time was no different from the rest because, after the group picked on him, calling him all types of punks and suckers, he gave in.

What really broke the camel's back though, was when Mike told him to stop acting like a faggot. "It ain't nothing wrong with getting your dick sucked once in a while." Mike started chuckling as he looked at the others, who were doing the same.

While the five youths were involved in a cipher discussing Heather, she was on the next block watching them. To her, it seemed like hours had passed since they last passed her by because in between this time, she had taken a hit. Now, she was fiending so bad that she couldn't think about anything other than getting high. "Damn! that would feel so good, right about now" she thought. Thinking about getting high is what made her walk up to the youths, who were engaged in a conversation about her at the time. Neither of them noticed her either until she started to talk.

"Ray-Ray, can I speak to you please?" she asked. You could look in her eyes and at her body movements and tell she was in need of a hit badly. She was twitching, and licking her lips a hundred times a minute, and her eyes were open wide with excitement.

Just by looking at her movements caused all of them to laugh. Instead of talking to her right in front of the group, Ray-Ray walked with her about three yards away. "What's the deal?" he asked, as she looked him up and down smiling.

She questioned, "Can I get a twenty piece on credit until I get my paycheck next week?"

Before he even thought to answer no, he thought to himself, *One of my commandments in the crack game is to never give a fiend credit because the chances of getting paid back is slim to none.* Thinking this over quickly, he replied, "Nah, I can't do it."

To Ray-Ray's surprise, Heather grabbed his arm firmly as he backed up, stating "I'll do anything you want me to do Ray-Ray, just give me a twenty."

Ray-Ray knew what she meant so he said, without any expression, "Yo, you have to hit all of us off."

At first she had doubts about this and said, "Come on, Ray-Ray" as if pleading "I'll do you, but not all of them." pointing at the group. Not even bothering to say anything else, he turned as if to walk away, but just as he reached the group, she whispered, "Okay, okay, but we have to meet someone in a half hour." The group did not pay her words any attention; they just walked off, knowing that she would follow.

The decision was made to go to the spot, which just around the corner. Once inside, the group all took turns having oral sex performed on them. After Little Daz had his turn, he walked out of the living room and into the back room where they kept the pit bull they used to guard the spot when they were on shift. Coming out the room with the pit leashed by a thick chain in tow, he walked into the living room with a devilish grin on his face.

Before anyone even noticed what he'd done, he stated, "You have to suck the dog off to if you want to get paid." All four of the fellas fell out laughing. Ray-Ray, Jah-Jah, and Mike were sitting on the couch. Shawn was standing in the middle of the floor with his pants down to his knees. Hearing what Little Daz said, he pulled out of her mouth, falling to his knees with uncontrollable laughter. It all sounded funny, but they all knew Little Daz was not joking about what he'd said. If everything were up to him, things would have happened differently. Luckily for her, it wasn't though, so she was in luck.

Heather, still on her knees looking at Ray-Ray said, "Nah, I ain't doing no fucking dog. Come on now, I ain't fiending that much!"

Cutting her off before she could say anything else, Ray-Ray reached into his pocket, pulling out a little one-inch-sized baggie with a white rock in it. Throwing it to her he replied, "Take this shit and get out of here."

As she closed the door behind her, Little Daz said, "You seen her, she had cum all in her hair and on her shirt. She didn't even bother to ask for a towel or anything to wipe herself off. She just got up and bounced like nothing happened.

"Y'all should have let the dog get some, word." Again they were all over each other laughing hysterically.

"You're crazy!" Jah-Jah said as he rolled over laughing with the others.

Heather left the spot swaying from side to side down the strip, and as if like clock work, a red 318I BMW pulled over to the curb next to her. Driving the car was an older white man, who obviously knew her by the way they spoke to one another through the passenger window. All the while she was talking to him; Heather was wiping her hair with her hands as if she was trying to smooth it out. After talking a minute or so she got in on the passenger side before the driver pulled off, making a right turn at the corner.

At about the time all of this was going on, King had just come from a club out in Nassua County called "The Rock," and was driving on Sunrise Highway in Infinite's J30 Infiniti. Since it was somewhere around one in the morning and there were hardly any cars out, he did 100 miles an hour all the way to the Amityville exit. Cruising all the way, the car felt like it was gliding.

Driving down Albany Avenue at the normal speed limit, King was feeling relaxed and he just lay back, enjoying the fact that he was almost home. Coming within two blocks of where he lived, as the Infiniti approached the corner stopping at a stop sign, a cop car was passing on the opposite side of the street. King and the officer looked one another in the face as the cars passed one another. Simultaneously, the lights flicked on the top of the police vehicle and the sirens went on as the driver made a full turn to get in back of King. King noticed right away and thought, *this shit can't be happening,* but it was. For a minute, he was hoping it was a dream. Luck wasn't with him tonight though because everything was the real thing, down to every split second.

Once King came to a full stop, the police cruiser pulled in back of him. Butterflies started to flutter in his stomach, and for some reason, he knew the situation involved more than a traffic violation. Looking through the rearview mirror, he could see the police officer stepping out of the vehicle.. Every sound seemed to echo in his brain like it was amped up ten times over: the sound of the siren, the door slamming, even the beast's foot steps approaching the driver's side of the car. The officer asked him "Is this your vehicle?"

"Nah. It's a family members"

"Can I see your license and registration?" the officer then asked.

King's intuition proved him right about the situation. It definitely led to something more than a traffic violation. Reaching over to the glove compartment he fumbled with the lock, taking a little while to open it, and retrieved the paperwork to hand it over.

The officer walked over to his patrol car, reaching through the window, grabbing the CB to call in the verification of the ID while looking ahead at the car in front of his. He must have called for back up as well because within a minute or so, another cruiser pulled up in back of his. After speaking with this officer for what seemed to be thirty seconds, he started to walk up towards King's car with the other officer in tow. Just seeing the other vehicle pull up shook King up, but now that they were both approaching, he was even more worried. All he heard was "Sir, you have a warrant for your arrest. Can you please step up out of your vehicle?"

At first, what the officer stated did not register in King's mind. So the officer asked again, "Sir, step out of the vehicle." His hand held firmly around the Glock at his waist. After taking the key out the ignition, King stepped out, slowly placing his outstretched hands on top of the car while the officer patted him down. In these days and times, when police arrest someone, they hardly ever read one their "Miranda Rights" to let them know their rights after being arrested. Instead, they just throw the handcuffs on and take you away. And this day was no different. Placing King in the back seat of the cruiser, the police officer stepped in on the drivers' side and sped off to the precinct.

The look on King's face was of an individual who was totally confused. He was scared to say the least because this was the first time he'd ever been arrested. *What the fuck did they want him for?* was the question he asked himself over and over again. One thing was for sure, he wasn't gonna go down by himself. This he knew for sure, he'd do whatever was necessary to get out of whatever trouble he was in. He had better things to do with his life than go to jail.

Chapter Six

T he two detectives stood outside the window of the interrogation room-watching King. They were wondering what they should do with him. Should they let him go? Or should they detain him until the two suspects were apprehended? After contemplating this for about ten minutes, in the end they decided to let him go, just in case his buddies became suspicious of his sudden disappearance. There was no telling what these guys were capable of. This fact was verified by the guy who slipped into unconsciousness for a couple of hours after being hit with the butt of the gun several times in his face and head. Luckily, he wasn't killed. Better yet, and luckily for the detectives, he was able to recall who it might have been. With this second witness, this criminal underground ring in Suffolk County was about to go under, for sure. All the detectives could think about were the promotions that were going to come when all the smoke cleared. Yes, it was going to be glorious.

All across Long Island, raids were being conducted simultaneously, and within an hour's time, 50 people had been rounded up.

Down the block from Infinite's home, a squad of twenty officers, all geared in black fatigues and heavily armed, prepared to storm his home and take him into custody, dead or alive. All they awaited now was the green light to go ahead with the operation.

Inside Infinite's home, all occupants inside were oblivious to what was taking place outside. Inside one room, four naked women stood along rectangular tables scaling and bagging cocaine. Twenty-eight grams were placed in each baggie and set up in piles of ten. In the living room, Infinite, Takim, and Kariem sat in a area of couches positioned in a half circle around a forty-eight-inch screen watching an x-rated movie. In the master bedroom, which was next to the room where the girls were bagging up, there were the two brothers "Knowledge" and "Knowledge-Knowledge," who were always together. They sat on the end of each side of the bed cleaning their semi-automatic weapons. One had a Desert Eagle 9mm, and the other a 45. They were serious about their business, so therefore, they treated their weapons like one would treat something that was precious to them.

Knowledge had the instincts of a wild animal. For some reason, he just felt a presence. It was like he smelled danger; to him; it was a lingering aroma that now existed. Always true to himself, he told his brother, "Yo, god I'm a go outside and walk around and make sure everything's culture. His frame was of a man who worked out constantly and ate the right foods. He was solid muscle, not to mention the fact that he was 6'4. He walked out the bedroom door, ducking his head down and twisting his body to get through. He walked down the hallway with the Desert Eagle in his right hand by his side. He turned the corner and walked into the living room, which was where the front door was. With only one foot into the living room, the front door came crashing open, splintering wood and pieces of the lock all over. Instantly, Knowledge swung around the corner, but not before letting his Glock spit bursts of fire into the first fatigued figure that sought to come into the house, sending his frame twirling backwards falling onto the porch with a thump. His fellow officers desperately fought back, firing aimlessly into every angle of the large structure. By this time, Infinite, Takim, and Kariem had also pulled out and started firing their weapons out the window frames naked of glass. All that could be heard were gunfire and women screaming. Both sounds echoed off the wall in unison.

Within seconds, the house was surrounded with squadrons of fatigued police units who were exchanging gunfire with Infinite and his Brotherhood comrades. Takim was the first one to get shot. Two slugs hit him in his face, sending him falling to the ground without an utter or scream. It's a matter of fact, he fell neither frontward nor backwards. Instead, he fell as if his legs just gave up on him. Neither Kariem nor Infinite noticed; they were too busy trying to save their own lives.

A fairly rock-like object came soaring through the open front doorway and as it hit the ground, smoke was released from the weapon on both sides of the line. Infinite screamed to Kariem "Let's try to make it out to the back rooms!" With this said, they both crawled while at the same time, firing back out of the house. Infinite reached the hallway throughout the struggle, but Kariem didn't. Instead, Kariem lay on the ground motionless, with his gun lying on the floor but still being held firmly by his grip.

Inside the master bedroom, the two brothers were going crazy firing their weapons as if they really believed they could take on the whole task force. As ferocious and skilled as the pair was, they were no match for the brute opposing force of the U.S. government. Within minutes, they were picked off by police snipers, leaving the air filled with no more gun fire, only the sobs and screams of women, the sound of police CB's, and officers giving orders to their subordinates.

Entering the house carefully, a team of ten task force members took position as they stepped slowly through the war torn house, with guns pointed out forward. Once the women were found, teams were set up to sift through the house to make sure that there were no assailants left.

Infinite laid flat on his stomach with his gun by his side in a 3 by 6 foot compartment built in the ceiling of the bathroom. The compartment was not built to hide anything or for secrecy, so the door was noticeable to anyone who walked into the bathroom.

For what seemed to be an hour, the team searched through the house without any clue as to his whereabouts until it was made certain that his body was not one of the casualties found. Had it not been that the authorities were specifically looking for him, he probably would have been safe where he was.

"Bring the dogs in here," Sergeant Cromier, who was in charge of this unit yelled into his CB. Within seconds, four officers came in with German Shepards, dragging them all around the house. As one German Shepard reached the hallway just about 3 yards from the bathroom, it started to bark, dragging the officer towards the bathroom and then into it, damn near leaping up to the ceiling. Infinite, hearing this, released himself through the compartment doors, falling out of the ceiling and at the same time firing. The dog and officer were instantly murdered. As Infinite hit the tiled floor, the Glock dropped from his hand. Hurt, he tried to rush and grab hold of the gun, but bullets kept raining into the bathroom, hitting him about thirty times before leaving his frame sprawled in the corner stuck in between the toilet bowl and bath tub.

As Infinite and his comrades' bodies were being taken away from the house, Blaze was already in custody, being booked on four counts of 1st degree armed robbery and attempted murder. He was snatched up without a struggle while he walked out of his girlfriend's apartment. At the moment he placed the key into the door of his car, a cold blunt object was placed to his head. Before he could think to turn around, a voice stated "Blaze, don't move you're under arrest!"

At the same time, a Crown Victorian pulled up in front of his car. Two detectives jumped out with gats outstretched in his direction. Looking at the detectives ahead of him, Blaze realized that this meant the end of freedom as he knew it for a while. All he could do was shake his head. He wasn't even aware of the detective with the gat to him, ordering him to place his hands shoulder-width, straight up in the air.

"Place your heads up in the air slowly. Drop the keys to the ground while you do this, and then move up towards the car with your chest touching it," the detective ordered. Doing as he was told, Blaze was then frisked from top to bottom, before his hands were placed behind his back and his wrists were handcuffed.

After placing Blaze in the back of the Crown Victorian, the two detectives got in the front. As the car pulled off, Blaze looked up towards his girlfriend's apartment. Because of the manner in which his arrest had occurred, she would not know what happened to him until the next morning. Right now it didn't matter to Blaze, his freedom was on the line and that was his main concern; everything else was small and minute at that very moment.

By this time, Blaze's friends were being taken away in body bags to the morgue. Although he did not know it, the detectives were fully aware of this. Turning his head for a second towards Blaze, one detective looked ahead into the streets, oblivious to what was going on in the car. The detective driving the car tried to get Blaze's attention by saying," Blaze, I'm Detective Richard, and this is Detective Avis Winsten, help us out and we'll help you out. You're a young guy. What are you seventeen or something?" He paused, as if waiting for a reply.

Not uttering a word, Blaze just nodded. He wasn't in the mood for bullshit from the beast who he knew was trying to run psychological games on him. As a matter of fact, he felt like going to rest at the moment. The reality of the situation drained him of all his strength and awareness. Slipping back into consciousness he heard, "We know all about your little syndicate, Infinite, MPR, the whole drug and robbery operation. It seems you guys had this county bagged up. But y'all made one fuck up," smiling to himself and pausing before going on, he added, "that was when you messed with Boom, who is in good standing with us.

"If it wasn't for that mistake, things probably would have been great for y'all for several years. But, mistakes will get you all the time." Stopping in mid sentence, he scratched his head with his right hand while holding the steering wheel with the left as if contemplating before continuing. "Yeah, mistakes is what keeps me getting a paycheck every week." Letting these thoughts settle in, Detective Richard kept driving without saying anything else the whole way to the precinct. Besides, Blaze would not have heard him anyway, because he dozed off while the detective was somewhere between sentences. In two different places at one time, miles away from one another, two individuals sat alone. Both felt tense, and a little scared, to be honest, because they both were the cause of what was taking place on the TV screen at that moment.

On the 11:30 PM. news a special bulletin was being posted. The news report started off with a spokesman in the police department surrounded by five staff members standing around a podium explaining what had taken place in the department's view of the situation. The spokesman started off by saying, "All throughout the hours of today, one of the most powerful and influential street crime operations was cracked down on. As the operation was unfolding, the lives of four officers were lost, due to the retaliation of gang members belonging to an organization called the Brotherhood. Over fifty-six members were arrested and detained on various charges ranging from drug and weapons possession to murder. We were not able to apprehend all suspects involved in the ring, so therefore we ask that anyone who has any information as to the whereabouts of any more members, please call us at the following hotline." At that moment, the phone number came across the screen in bold white lettering before the bulletin was discontinued and the regular news resumed.

Boom and King were two different individuals in two different places, yet they both had a lot in common at the moment. King sat upright on the end of his bed while Boom lay in his hospital bed with his head bandaged up to the point where just his eyes, nose, and mouth showed. Both were glued to the TV as if there lives depended on it. Neither one, at the moment, was feeling well; probably because neither of them felt safe. They both knew their lives were in the balance at the moment. King was fully aware of the extent of what went down, since he furnished the information that struck the deadliest blows to the family. He knew for a fact that if this got out, he was going to be murdered without question. Boom, on the other hand, was scared because he didn't know whether Infinite was connected.

It was about three or four o'clock in the early morning before either of the two could go to sleep. King's stomach was bothering him all night with sharp pains and bubbling motions, so he practically stayed in the bathroom. Boom was bedridden due to his physical state. He felt the same as King, but was forced to defecate on himself. The nurses would have to clean him up when the 6 o'clock morning shift came on.

* * * * *

"Mrs. Davis, is this she?" the voice on the other end asked.

"Yes it is. Who's speaking?" Beverly asked as butterflies began to swell up in her stomach.

"Ma'am, I am detective James and I'm sorry to inform you that Derrik—"

Before he could continue, Beverly cut him off screaming hysterically. "No! No! No!" sobs ripped through her. "No! No! Not my baby!" She fell to the floor with phone still in hand.

The gentleman on the other end called out, "Mrs. Davis, Mrs. Davis." But all he could hear was a bunch of no's before the line clicked off.

Beverly had waited for this day to come. She would have nightmares about receiving this call about her only son, whom she loved so much. She only threw him out because she just could not be around him and watch him throw his life away.

* * * * *

"Mommy, stop-bugging, Blaze is not any member of a gang or something like that," pausing for a moment seeking the right words to continue Rachel added, "He probably knew them guys. And you know how them people are, they figure all black guys are involved in some gang or something, or that you have to be involved in one just because you know somebody in one. Mommy, plus, I love him, and I'm a grown woman so don't go on worrying about me, I'll be okay." she said, as if reassuring herself as well.

"Well, baby I guess you know what you're doing. And like you said, you're grown. But, if you need me, you know that I'm here for you always."

Smiling and thinking about how much she loved her mom, Rachel told her "I know, mom, but I love him and he loves me, so I have to stick by him."

They talked a little while longer, exchanging small talk, gossip, and stuff like that before saying, " I love you," to one another and hanging up the phone.

After hanging up, Rachel took a deep breath, and then placed both of her hands on the top of her head, interlocking all ten fingers together. Her concentration was very deep, as if she were meditating. She was thinking of Blaze, wondering how he was doing and if he was thinking of her like she was thinking of him.

Why did he have to be so stubborn anyway? She thought to herself. She had told him time after time that his getting locked up was bound to happen if he continued to pursue the lifestyle he was living. But he would always brush her off stating, "Rachel, I came from nothing, and I'm never trying to go back there. I'd rather be dead than broke and penniless."

She missed him more than ever at that moment; and the more she thought about it, the more she just wanted to cry. Yet she knew if Blaze were around, he would frown on such a thing. He always told her that in desperate times one needed to be strong, and that tears did nothing but weaken the soul. Thinking of this brought a smile to her face.

She would never leave him no matter what happened, she vowed to herself. She knew that from the first time they slept together. He wasn't her first, but she knew he was the first guy who truly made love to her, satisfying her in every way like never before.

After waking up out of her thoughts, a feeling of fatigue came over her. Walking out of the kitchen into the bedroom, she decided to take a bubble bath. Standing in front of the six-foot mirror on her bedroom wall, Rachel started to undress. As she did this, she thought of how many times she and Blaze played this scene out. He would undress her, then kiss and caress her from head to toe as she watched in the mirror. Just thinking about it almost gave her an orgasm. *Oooh!* she thought. *Why did you have to get locked up?*

Thinking back on the first time the mirror episode happened caused Rachel to blush. Once all her clothing was off, Blaze would stand in back of her while their two bodies pressed against one another tightly. As both of his hands cupped her breasts, his manhood pressed against her. He kissed and nibbled on her neck, sending a tickling sensation down her spine. Her eyes were closed, so he smacked her on her butt causing it to sting with irritation. To this she asked, "What?" And his order was for her to keep her eyes glued on the mirror and to watch what he was doing. She was so shy, but at the same time he had her so open and horny that she started enjoying what he was doing to her. Even more once she continued watching in the mirror. He kissed her from head to toe on her backside before stepping in front of her and into the space between her and the mirror. This time, he did the same to the front of her while he cupped her breasts. She must have came at least three times without him even penetrating her.

Snapping up out of her thoughts once again, Rachel looked at herself once more. Her nipples were hard and practically pulsating. Looking down, she could see wetness all around her crotch, and cum dripping down her inner thighs. She felt exhausted, yet hornier than ever. Turning away from the mirror and touching her breasts as she walked, she thought about how wonderful a bubble bath was going to feel, and how much she needed it so bad to relax herself. How was she going to be able to see Blaze today, and not be able to get none? *Damn, I'm a have to buy a toy*, she told herself.

Dipping herself into the bathtub, Rachel sunk her whole body under the suds, just barely leaving her head on the surface "Ahh, it feels so gooood!" she coed before slipping into a relaxed state.

****

On tier four-west – north in Riverhead Correctional Facility, the C.O. called out Jermaine Jackson on the attorney visit. Once cell number ten was cracked, it took Blaze about a minute to throw a green shirt on, along with a pair of county slip on sneakers.

Stepping up out of the cell with his green uniform, Blaze felt naked and out of place.

"What a nightmare," he mumbled to himself as he walked past the first nine cells towards the front gate.

The tier was overwhelmed with noise, and since Blaze was only eighteen, he was situated on the adolescent tier, which at the time was on twenty-three hour lock-in because of the violence that permeated the gallery on a regular basis.

Blaze knew three of the fellas who were on the gallery. Therefore, when he came in, from the jump, he was accepted without having to fight and prove himself, which was usually the norm when one came in, especially if they came in with foot wear that someone liked and wanted. The outcome of the fight would determine who kept the sneakers.

As Blaze walked up to the front of the tier past cell number two, his man Puerto Rican Born, who was the brother of one of his ex-girlfriends called out to him. "Yo! Blaze what's the deal? Who are you going to see?" he asked smiling.

Shaking his head as if in disbelief, Blaze replied, "Yeah, I'm going to see this guy. He better have something good to tell me god, for real." After stating this, he could see that the C.O. had come back onto the floor and was waiting for him so he told Born "Peace!" holding up the peace sign as he bounced.

Walking up to the gate, the C.O. asked with an attitude, "Are you Johnson?"

Blaze replied, "Yeah."

Looking him up and down with scowl on his face the C.O. placed the key into the lock, turning it to unlock the steel, barred door. Once Blaze came out the C.O. closed the door. As it slammed, making a loud noise like two pieces of steel being thrown together, he placed the key back in the door once again, but this time locking it. Directing Blaze to stand towards the side with his hands against the wall, he frisked him before telling him to go stand in the elevator platform out in the lobby.

Out in the lobby, there was a C.O. and a sergeant seated at a desk talking shit and carrying on. Neither of them paid him any mind as he walked in. The only attention that was given to him was when the sergeant told him to stand over by the elevator door and wait until an officer came up in the elevator to escort him.

Hearing the elevator approaching the floor caused Blaze to turn around and look, "ching-ching" rang out the sound of the elevator as it reached its destination. As the doors opened an officer stood asking Blaze where he was going. After Blaze informed him, the officer directed him toward the back of the elevator and then the doors closed, sending the elevator three floors down to the first floor. As he got out of the elevator trap, an officer turned, pointing a finger toward his right, letting Blaze know where to go.

Walking into the attorney visiting room, Blaze was frisked another time before being allowed to walk into the visiting area. As he sat waiting alone at the table, he surveyed his surroundings. Inside the area were four little rooms. The guard had directed him to the first one on the left and told him to take a seat inside until his attorney showed up. It was not a long wait because within minutes, a slim dapper figure stepped in the room and sat across from Blaze. He held out his right hand to Blaze, smiling and exhibiting bright white, even rows of teeth. "Hey, Mr. Johnson, my name is Mr. Rayne. I represent all of your friends. I was retained a long time ago to represent you if you ever got into trouble.

"Oh! And by the way, I'm sorry to hear about your friends, Mr. Rome and the rest" He said all of this as if he was really sincere about what he was saying.

Blaze had no idea what the man was talking about so he asked, "Sorry about what? Getting locked up sometimes is part of the game, right?"

Waiting for a reply, he searched the attorney's eyes to see what angle he was coming from. But at that very moment, it occurred to the attorney that Blaze might not know of the incident because he got arrested around the same time that the situation had taken place. The attorney carefully decided he would have to tell. Taking a deep breath while at the same time looking up in the air, he went on.

"Mr. Johnson, your friend Derrik and some of your other friends were killed yesterday. They had a shoot out with the police at a house located on Marbury Street as the police sought to bring them in on a warrant." He wanted to continue but thought against it because the look on Blaze's face told him that the kid had heard enough. Anger was written all over his face. Inside, Blaze felt badly injured. Mentally, it was if the whole world came crashing down upon him.

"I must stay strong," he reminded himself. Plus, he didn't know this man in front of him well enough to let him see his true feelings. For what seemed a minute or so of deep contemplation with his forehead surfaced in the palm of his hands. He started to speak, looking the attorney square in the face.

"So where does that leave me with this case?" By this calmness on his part Blaze left the attorney in a state of utter surprise, to the point where when he first tried to speak, the words did not come out. But then he got it right.

"Well, Mr. Johnson, considering the circumstances surrounding this case and the little circumstantial evidence that the authorities do have, it puts you in good standing, to say the least. We have two statements, one by Terrence Jones who claims he had an argument with Derrik in the parking lot of a flea market. He claims that later Derrik robbed him and his wife at gunpoint. And then we also have a statement by Mr. Isaiah Rome, who happens to be Derrik's cousin. His street name is King, do you know him?" He asked, staring at Blaze intently.

Blaze pushed his face into a frown, placing his hands into a balled up fist on the table unknowingly. "Yeah, I know that faggot, he's supposed to be family."

With a smirk on his face, the attorney continued, "Well, it's obvious that he did not feel the same about you, Derrik, nor the company y'all kept because he gave explicit details of who's who and the daily operations of the so-called Brotherhood establishment; specifically implicating you and Derrik. But because of what happened to Derrik yesterday, this case for you becomes that much easier to beat. We'll get around everything though, and I'm a try to get your bail reduced at the bail reduction hearing next week, so we'll get you out." Without another word, he got up and reached over, outstretching his right hand to Blaze.

"Stay out of trouble, okay." This was more of a statement than a plea, and Blaze knew exactly what he meant. He was already facing enough and didn't need anything else.

After the attorney left, Blaze remained seated. All he could think about was how both King and Boom were going to pay for their loose lips.

"Weak ass mother fuckers," he whispered to himself. At that moment, all types of devious thoughts were going through his head. Visions of Infinite and him as kids playing flashed in his mind. One thing was for sure; he knew they both had to pay for their cowardice, which is the reason why his friends were dead. As he slapped both of his palms on the desk, the guard came in.

"Johnson, you can go to your tier now." Once up on the fourth floor, he had to go back to his cell, since the tier was in twenty-three hour lockdown. He kicked off his sneakers and jumped under the covers without even bothering to take off his clothes. Hearing Blazes cell lock, Puerto Rican Born called out to him.

"Yo, god what happened?" Blaze did not really want to be bothered, but figured a little conversation was not going to hurt him, so he sat up with the covers still around him.

"It's all good, god. I should be getting out next week, once my bail gets reduced."

Born knew about what had happened to Infinite and figured maybe it was okay to speak on it now that Blaze had time to think on the situation. "Yo, Gee, I'm sorry to hear about Infinite, that was a real nigga, for real!" pausing for a couple of seconds he added, "Me and him go way back to the neighborhood store, word." he said this with a tone of such sincerity that Blaze could tell that the man really felt love for this brother Infinite, and that he was truly bothered by what happened.

For a minute, Blaze almost started to cry, but he held back the urge, stating "Yeah, that was my strength, yo, he was my partner and brother, gee…shit, ain't gonna be the same without him, god. He was the realest out of all my peeps."

He couldn't even talk anymore without getting mad, so he told Born, "Yo, god, I'll speak to you later," before lying back down to contemplate some more. Since it was only eleven in the morning, almost everyone was still asleep. It wasn't long before Blaze dozed off into deep consciousness.

***

Coming out of her apartment, Rachel noticed that it was a nice day. The sun was beaming brightly. Already at twelve in the afternoon, it had to be at least eighty degrees, she thought. Everything about the day just seemed beautiful to her, yet things were not perfect at all. Thinking of Blaze put a damper on the day.

Rachel had to walk over to her car, which was parked in a space four apartments down. As she began to walk, she heard loud voices and screams of a man and woman arguing, and from the conversation, language that they were using, and all the noise that went along with it, Rachel just knew that they were into something serious.

The window screen to the apartment where the man and woman were at must have been open because anyone outside could hear every word uttered clearly. As Rachel approached the apartment on her way to the car she heard, " Bitch, what the fuck! Didn't I tell you that if I caught you I was gonna kill you?"

After that, all that was heard was a slap and sobs, and then some tussling before the door swung open. A woman ran out, stumbling out the doorway, tripping as she hit the concrete, while the crazed man chased behind her screaming and swearing. Although she tripped, she caught her step right away, picking up the pace and running right into Rachel, who could not avoid the crash. Rachel damn near flew into the wall, while the woman just kept running for her dear life as the man continued to chase her. Rachel felt sorry for the woman at first, but after practically being run over, she now felt like cursing out the both of them.

Rachel stood for a minute to catch her breath as she watched the two run down the avenue in frenzy. Once they were out of sight she fixed her summer dress, pulling it down tightly around herself. After approving of how she looked, Rachel stepped on so she could do what she had started to do in the first place.

Reaching the car, a new Toyota Camry, she pressed the automatic unlocking system on her key chain and got in "Wooooooh!" she exclaimed, because the car interior was sticky and hot. Without hesitating for one moment, she quickly started the ignition, turning the air condition on full blast. As she pressed the automatic control on the driver's door panel her seat tilted back and then she pulled the seat strap around her, placed the gear into reverse and backed out..

Coming to a stop at the end of the block, Rachel threw "Big Punisher" into the cassette deck. She was singing along with the chorus, practically dancing in the seat as if she was in a club or party.

On the way to the jail, all Rachel could think about was how Blaze was doing. She couldn't wait to see him. *There's no need to worry,* she thought to herself as she drove. She decided not to even think about it. She'd find out the answer to her question soon enough.

A half an hour later, she drove into the parking lot of the Riverhead Correctional Facility. She had to first stop at a Sheriff's checkpoint booth. As she pulled up next to the window, the deputy asked for her license and registration before letting her enter the compound.

Inside the waiting area, all visitors had to fill out a sign up sheet as they entered. It was about 12:10 PM and the visiting hours started at 1:00 PM, so she had to sit and wait. The wait wasn't too much of a hassle because, she quickly befriended a Spanish girl named Rosa, who was also waiting to see her man. They gossiped for the remaining time, until visitor's names started being called out by the guard.

By then, it was 12:50 and the guard had begun to call out names. Once their names were called, both Rachel and Rosa were deaf to the names that were called after theirs. As they bounced up from their seats with anticipation and joy, they almost did not hear the officer tell anyone to line up behind the metal detector.

No pocket books, accessories or jewelry, except for wedding bands, were permitted to be worn by any visitors in the visiting room. Therefore, everyone was given a lock and placed their valuables inside a locker before passing through the metal detectors.

When Rachel stepped into the visiting room, she was told by the officer stationed there to sit at number nineteen. Even though the room was already half way packed, she picked Blaze out of the pack right away. He was waving at her, which caused him to stand out even more. Once their eyes connected, smiles flooded their faces all at once. Approaching the bench where he stood at, Rachel reached across the 3-inch high divider that was on top of the table to hug him; they embraced one another, kissing furiously before letting go.

They sat looking into the glass smiling at one another for about two minutes, without even saying a word. Blaze was the first to start up a conversation "So how's my baby doing?"

Rachel smiled stating, "I'm okay, but I miss you like crazy. When are you coming home to me? Your mom is coming up tomorrow. She's mad as hell with you. She was crying about Infinite, but at the same time, she's glad you're alive. She told me to tell you that she loves you. She said to also tell you that you changed into what she was trying to keep you from turning into."

Still smiling without breaking a bit Blaze went on, "The lawyer came this morning. He said I should be out next week when they drop my bail."

Rachel almost laughed with joy upon hearing this, tears started to form in her eyes. Blaze's facial expression was the total opposite; it changed to sadness as he mentioned the rest.

"That's the good news, the bad news is that Infinite, Kariem, and Takim got killed yesterday by the police about the same time they arrested me...that shit's fucked up, right?"

Rachel knew how close Blaze was to them, so hearing this news filled her with sadness, even though she already knew. To see him in this unhappy state made her unhappy as well. All she could think to do after hearing the news was to hold both of her hands to her face and say, "Oh my god!" as she looked into Blaze's eyes to see what he was feeling.

Blaze was happy to see her, so he didn't want to dampen the moment by utilizing the whole visit speaking on things that were negative. Therefore, he took the conversation to another level, besides death and prison. They talked so much that the hour visit seemed like only twenty minutes. As Rachel left, Blaze thought about telling her about King but decided against it. King's situation would remain his little secret. He'd take care of King his way. The code of the streets would deal with him promptly.

Chapter Seven

N ow that Takim and Kariem were not alive anymore, Freedom, Jasheem, and Divine took over MPR and from day one, after the news circulated about what happened, they began facing opposition from a Jamaican posse from Queens called Roots.

Neither crew was making money now that they had been at war for three weeks.

The whole terrace strip was like a ghost town at night. Not a soul could be heard of or seen on the streets in the late night hours. If you did see anyone, you can bet that nine out of ten times, they were holding heat. The body count was already five people dead, three from the posse, one from MPR, and one innocent by standard, who was a girlfriend of one of the Jamaicans. Nothing personal, she was simply a casualty of war. She just happened to be on the driver's side while her boyfriend was on the passenger's side getting gunned down as they stopped for a red light.

The war started when one of the members of Roots aired Little Daz out with three shots to his upper chest with a nine-millimeter. The night after Takim and Kariem had been murdered, the Jamaicans had moved their spot diagonally across from MPR's spot. Normally their spot was two blocks down from MPR's because everyone had established territory in the area. Now the West Indians, feeling that MPR was not a threat anymore, decided to move their spot closer.

Usually everything was culture and cool between the two crews, but that night the Jamaicans decided to make a power move.

In their eyes MPR was nothing without Takim and Kariem, who were known for busting their guns whenever drama was present. Freedom, Jasheem and Divine were the pretty boy types, who were known for their ability to get girls and money.

All the drama started on Little Daz, Shawn, Ray–Ray, Mike, and Jah–Jah's shift. That night, since it was raining outside, Ray–Ray, Shawn, and Jah–Jah clad out in rain gear, all took turns serving the customers, instead of just Ray–Ray and Jah–Jah as usual, while Little Daz, Shawn, and Mike ran the inside of the spot, taking care of the security, counting the money, bagging up the material, and distributing it. Freedom would always come before closing to take care of the books, calculate how much material was sold, and how much money was made.

It was raining so bad and was so dark outside that one could hardly see people within a ten a ten-foot radius; everything appeared as shadows. One of the crack heads had told Jah–Jah that the Jamaicans were moving in on MPR's territory and were selling three buildings down, across from them. To make matters worse, they were selling ten dollar pieces, while MPR were selling twenty dollar pieces. To make a long story short, not only were the Jamaicans moving in an MPR'S territory but they also were selling the same quantity of the product to the friends for a cheaper price, which meant that they were cutting MPR'S throat.

Hearing about the situation from Jah–Jah, Little Daz and Mike started flipping and decided to step to their business. Everything was supposed to be run by rules and regulations. When a problem occurred at the spot, the lieutenant, who in this case was Little Daz, was supposed to call one of the heads, so they could decide on what action should be taken about the matter at hand. But Little Daz had that "fuck that" mentality and attitude twenty-four hours, seven days a week. As water dripped off his rain gear onto the floor, Jah–Jah rushed toward the back room where Little Daz sat stacking the night's money into hundred dollar piles, so he could later stack them together in one thousand dollar piles and place rubber bands around them. Without knocking, Jah–Jah barged into the door sending it slamming back into the wall and causing it to make a thud noise as it did so. Before Jah–Jah was halfway into the room; Little Daz had his burner, a small .380, out and pointed directly at him, ready to rock. Jah–Jah was startled by Little Daz's reaction and for a minute, froze, until Little Daz placed the burner back onto the surface of the table and it made a "clank" sound.

"What's" the deal, god?" Daz asked, looking concerned. He knew something was wrong for Jah-Jah to just storm in, because normally he would knock.

Jah–Jah, standing soaked from head to toe with a look of irritation on his face started screaming, "Them fuckin', boomba clot Rasta mother fuckers are selling twenties for ten dollars, three buildings down!" Little Daz had a look in his face that said, "stop lying," but at the same time he picked up the .380 and stormed into the next room where Mike sat behind a table bagging packages.

"Yo, sun, them mother fuckin' root ass niggers down the block are tying to move on us, word is bond."

Mike knew exactly whom he was talking about, but didn't believe it himself, so he needed to hear it again. The shocked him so much that he had to stop what he was doing and ask, "What you talking about, god?"

Little Daz was so pissed off that he was practically walking in circles, cursing and mumbling to himself quietly as he held the .380 in his right hand and pointed it at the floor. In the background, Jah–Jah just stood in the doorway looking dumbfounded. Punching the wall, Little Daz yelled, "Them niggers got a spot three buildings down from us, selling ten dollar pieces cutting our throats!" He screamed so loud that his voice echoed off the walls.

For a minute, Mike just sat there without saying anything. Then he said, "Yo, gee, we have to call Freedom, Jasheem, or Divine."

Little Daz was at the boiling point cuz because it was not the first time he ran into problems with the Jamaican posse. There was no question what he wanted to do. So to Mike's reply he stated, "Man, fuck that, we're gonna step to these mother fuckers ourselves, yo. They're pussy, frontin' like their some type of murderers or something." Pausing for a second to think about what else to say, he went on, "Them fagots ain't killin' nothing!"

Without even saying anything else, he stormed out of the room, and went back into the room where he was geared up into rain gear. Just as little Daz was about to bounce out of the room, Mike came in and said, "God, let's see what's the deal with these clowns." Mike really felt they should call one of the bosses first, but at the same time, he was not going to let Little Daz go handle the business by himself. Whatever happened would have to happen to the both of them. Opening the front door to the spot, a gush of wind hit him. Little Daz was so mad that nothing would have bothered him at the moment. Rage was sketched out all over his face. Standing on the first step of the balcony, Little Daz just looked at Mike, turning his head for a brief second before stepping down the steps in a bop with Mike only two or three feet behind him. Both had their hands positioned inside their raincoat pockets. Little Daz held his fingers around the.380 in his right pocket tightly, making sure to be careful not to pull the trigger unnecessarily because he knew the safety lever was off. The last thing he wanted to do was shoot himself or an innocent by standard. Mike's 9 millimeter Glock was positioned inside the waist line of the pants he wore under his rain trousers.

Reaching the bottom of the steps, both of their boots made a splashing sound as they stepped into a big puddle. Jah–Jah, Ray–Ray, and Shawn could be seen in the distance by the green rain gear they wore. Customers in the distance were looking in their direction. Little Daz yelled through the stormy window and rain, "Hold it down, god! We'll be right back!"

Jah–Jah could be seen holding something up. Little Daz figured it was his arm, letting him know that he heard what he said. Little Daz crossed the street with Mike alongside him. The rain was coming down so hard that even through they wore rain suits; it still felt cold and damp, like they were donning diver's suits underwater. The sound the rain made hitting the ground was similar to music on a CD; it was very clear and precise, drowning out everything else. Stepping onto the concrete, a figure could be seen barely through the dark buckets of rain, Little Daz mention for Mike not to say anything by placing his right hand towards his month for a brief second before putting it back in his the pocket of his raincoat, and retrieving the .380 which was already cocked off safety and ready to rock. At that moment, Mike also pulled out his weapon. He was nervous as hell, and for and minute wished that he hadn't come but called the bosses instead so they could handle the situation. It was too late to think about that now, he told himself as he watched Little Daz walk up on one of the figures with the .380 at his side.

"What the fuck y'all doing?" Little Daz yelled, gripping the .380 tightly.

"What ya deal wit' stah" was all that was heard from the figure as gunshots came from out of one of the cars parked along the street just in front of the figure and Little Daz. All Mike saw were little balls of flames and smoke, as water and stream surrounded the atmosphere. Little Daz's body jerked and then twirled around like a ballerina as the gun he held flew to the ground, making several clank sounds as it scattered across the concrete. Mike was so dazed that he watched Little Daz's body thump to the ground, before even thinking about busting his gun at the car, or figuring out who was standing near Little Daz a minute before. The shadow had taken flight into the ever present darkness ahead, as the car pulled off, simultaneously sending a stream of bullets in its path. Little Daz laid flat on his face at the end of the aftermath. Scared as hell, Mike ran back across the street to the safety of the spot. He approached, breathing heavily, not even aware of whether Little Daz was alive or not. Ray-Ray, Jah-Jah, and Shawn surrounded him. By this time, the rain had slowed down to a light drizzle.

"What the fuck happened? Where's Little Daz? Is he dead? Where the fuck is he at?"

These are the questions that he heard in repetition from the group. He felt like fainting, and in fact was not aware that he was sitting on the stoop shivering and damn near crying. Mike was oblivious to everything around him; nothing could reach him at that moment.

The three adolescents were hysterical with questions and anger. They screamed at him continuously. When this didn't work they then began to scream at one another, trying to figure out what to do.

"Fuck that, I'm goin' over there," yelled Shawn with his back turned toward the group already in motion towards where Little Daz lay. Looking at one another, and then at Mike, Ray-Ray and Jah-Jah decided to follow suit.

All three youths were strapped, holding their guns out in the air ready to bust a shot in any one of the Root members they saw, but none were around.

Shawn was the first one to come across Little Daz. Sobs ripped through his little frame as he turned his friend's body over to see the three open wounds that caused the pool of blood that now lay on the concrete mixed with water to look like Kool-Aid.. Blood was all over Sean's hands, and as Ray-Ray and Jah-Jah approached him kneeling next to the body, he stood up to contemplate, rubbing both bloody hands together.

One of the residents on the block, an old lady that everyone called Mama was looking out the window and saw the whole incident happen. Well, at least the part where Little Daz got shot. At the time, the rain was coming down too heavy for her to decipher who the culprits were shooting, or who, in fact, had gotten shot.

Mama, knew everyone's name who walked up and down the strip because all she did all day was look and listen from the window in her living room. She knew everything. Now that the rain had slowed down, she could now see the boy's figures. Right away, she knew they her children, as she liked to call them. Not that she gave birth to them, but seeing them doing their thing every day and walking up and down the strip enabled her to build a steady respectful relationship with the group. They all, in return, treated her with respect.

"Oh! My God" she exclaimed,, after seeing the group through the window. Running out the door without a raincoat caused her to shiver, but it didn't matter to her one bit because all she knew was that her children needed her.

Running down the steps to where the boys stood encircled around Little Daz's corpse, Mama jumped to the ground hugging the young man screaming, and sobbing. Tears the size of raisins streamed down her ebony face.

"He was just a boy! Just a little boy! Why? Why?"

Looking over to Ray-Ray, who seemed like the only one out of the three to have control over himself, she said as if in a daze, "Ray-Ray call the police! Call the police!" she kept saying this even as he was already in her house making the 911 call.

Within five minutes, a police car had pulled up to the curb next to the small group. Both front doors slammed leaving an enormous echo as the two officers stepped out of their cruiser and onto the curb. It was Frank and Speedy, two of the most known faces in the area. Frank was the neighborhood politician type, who most thought wouldn't be such a bad guy if it wasn't for the fact he was the beast. He knew every ones mom on the block. Sometimes if you had a warrant and he was cool with you, he'd tell you to go take care of it before his partner Speedy or one of the other beasts saw you. Speedy was the total opposite of his partner, an asshole devoted to his badge. To make matters worse, he could run like a track star. Everyone in the hood knew this and hated to see him on duty. Anytime he came on, the word would get around quicker than the plague. "Yo, gee Speedy is on, stay off the block."

Speedy loved the fact that everyone was scared of him. This was an honor because as a kid, he was the type everyone picked on. Even his father was ashamed of him for being the punk that he was as a kid, but his father just never found the heart to tell him so.

Reaching the group and looking down at Mama and the three young men, Frank took off his hat, holding it in his right hand as he asked Mama in a concerned voice, "Did you see who did this?"

All Mama could say was "No, I just heard gun shots and when I looked out my window, my little friend was just lying there."

There was nothing she could do but cry and pray that God took Little Daz into heaven, but for now, she would hold him until the ambulance came.

Hearing Mama's reply Frank now looked at the boys.

"Do any of you know why this happened?" Both cops were fully aware of what the youths were into. What a tragedy thought Frank. He wanted to help but how could one seek to help in a hopeless situation. He knew they weren't going to talk.

"Nah, we just heard gun shots and then Mama crying. That's why we ran over here. That is when we saw it was Little Daz." Ray-Ray said without looking the officer once in the face. Instead, his eyes stayed steadily fixed on the sidewalk.

A few minutes' later detectives and the crime scene investigative unit showed up. It wasn't until an hour later that Little Daz's body was picked up by paramedics and taken to the morgue. The ambulance left, leaving the bloodstains and the memory of Little Daz behind with the group standing on the pavement.

"Go home boys, it's three in the morning. Go home to your family." Frank told them before turning with his partner walking towards the police cruiser. The group stood talking as if they did not hear what he stated.

Pulling off the curb, as the car reached where the group stood, Speedy ducked his head out the window. "Go home," he said, as if giving an order.

"Fuck you!" Shawn replied, as the car sped off.

Speedy heard what was said, telling his partner "Did you hear that?"

Frank laughed saying, "Yeah, these are some tough kids." Pointing his finger he went on. "And I can bet you any amount of money that them little mother fuckers know exactly what happened to their friend." Holding his head with his right hand as he drove on, he added, "We're gonna have a fuckin' blood bath to deal with, no shit!"

Speedy didn't care what happened, his opinion was, "Fuck it, let the niggers kill each other." but he couldn't tell his do-good partner this. So he said, "It's all part of a day's work Frank. All part of a day's work. We're not God: all we can do is pick up the pieces."

All three youths sat on the couch in Mama's living room eating baked sugar cookies and drinking hot chocolate. Mama was done crying now, and it was her time to be strong. She loved these boys like her own, and wished she could take them all away from this hell they lived in called the ghetto. Mama was no dummy, she knew the youths sold drugs and was even aware that they carried guns. But in her eyes, they were just good boys caught up in a bad situation called life. Almost all of them came from a poor family, or one parent household, and some had no family at all, so the streets presented an easy option to take and was a place to connect with others and provide some type of family-like base.

As the trio ate, Mama just watched over them without saying a word. It wouldn't be long before they were back out there doing what they had to do, she thought to herself. She was absolutely right because a few moments later, Ray-Ray got up, walked over to her and hugged her tightly, telling her, "Mama, we have to go."

Looking up from their cups of hot chocolate, Jah-Jah and Shawn said, "Bye, Mama," before getting up and placing their cups down on the table. The large lady scooped them, along with Ray-Ray, up into her arms before they could escape out of the front door. She kissed them both on their foreheads while they squirmed in her grasp.

Walking out the doorway right away, the three spotted Freedom, Jasheem, and Divine's car along with a few others parked out in front of the spot. As the trio walked up onto the curb they could see Divine looking out of the window. He looked pissed, and they hoped that his anger was not towards them.

Stepping into the house they right away caught a glimpse of Mike, who was sitting in a chair in the middle of the living room while Divine, Jasheem, and some other cats all sat on couches which surrounded the perimeter of the living room. They were interrogating him to find out exactly what happened. Cautiously, the youngsters walked through the group. "Peace!" greeted them from their elders before Divine directed them towards the back room, which ironically was where Little Daz spent his last work hours, counting and calculating the night's earnings.

Gathering them all together, Divine stood in front of them with his tall, lanky frame towering over them like a skyscraper would to a project building. He was hurt by what had happened and needed to let them know that MPR was gonna handle their business concerning the situation.

Speaking as if in a whisper, he went on, "Yo, I want y'all to take a vacation for a month so we can handle things. You're still going to get paid your regular salary. But we just don't want y'all around. What happened to Little Daz is not going to go unanswered. Don't worry, word is bond, they're gonna feel it. That's all, yo. Every Friday, Jasheem will drop off all your pay to your cribs." Pausing to look directly at all of them, he continued, "When shit is cool and culture for y'all to come back to work, I'll personally scoop y'all up."

Divine was sincerely hurt by what happened to Little Daz, he couldn't even say anything else. He simply walked into the living room to join the rest of the fellas.

Ray-Ray, Jah-Jah, and Shawn were confused; they didn't know what they were going to do with themselves. Divine told them in so many words to just go home because there was nothing that they could do, but this did not settle to well with them. Looking at one another, they all walked down the hallway together. As they entered the living room, Divine said, "Yo, let me drop y'all off so y'all can stay off the streets. Mike is coming with y'all to hold y'all down." He would have felt bad if anything happened to one of them as they were leaving. Divine walked the group out the front door. With both hands placed inside the Columbia rain suit jacket, he gripped the nine-millimeter in his right pocket firmly. The expression on his face was blank and unexplainable. There was nothing left to do but go to war, he convinced himself.

The game is like that, if you're not willing to die or push someone's wig back to maintain your status to keep getting money, then you have no business in the game. Sooner or later, someone was going to press on you. It was all a part of the capitalistic way of life. A perfect example of this is the United States. It would not be the world power that it is today if it was not such a good player at the game of survival of the fittest. They extort nations, rob nations, bribe nations, and then, when all else fails, the military is used.

Thinking all this quietly to himself, Divine mumbled "What a life?"

Ray-Ray, who was just a step behind Divine, asked confused, "What?"

Divine just said, "Don't sweat it little god, just get in the car."

Divine had a new model Lincoln Continental, so there was no problem fitting all five of them in the car comfortably. They were all tired and ready to get out of there, so they rushed the car like linebackers rushing the line of scrimmage. Immediately, Divine started the car, taking it into drive without waiting for it to warm up. The youths were on their way home, and silently, each of them was happy to be alive at that moment.

***

Three days later, Little Daz's funeral was held. In all, there had to be about two hundred people present, about 70 of them were alone were affiliated with MPR. The rest were admirers and loved ones. As far as the Hempstead Terrace was concerned, he was ghetto superstar, and no one could deny this. Practically the whole neighborhood came out to show their love and pay their respects for the young cat.

Little Daz never knew of his father, so his absence at the funeral was to be expected. Even though his mother was a crack fiend and not much of a mother to him ever since she fell victim to the drug three years earlier, she cried continuously and talked in a mumbling crack-fit about how bad a mother she was to him and how she wished she could do it all over again. "Why didn't God take my life instead of his?" she cried, foaming from the mouth. Her raged fit went on all throughout the entire funeral service.

At the grave sight, the tension was so thick in the air that it was like a crime had just taken place on a busy street. People's faces were so sullen and filled with anger that hardly anyone spoke. If they did, it was just to say a few words in respect to their fallen friend.

All the old people wore traditional funeral garb, dark-colored suits and dresses. While the younger crowd came in their regular street gear, jeans, and baseball caps. It was definitely a gathering of his peers, for there were three times more young people present than elders.

Divine, Jasheem, and Freedom, along with most of the MPR team and its affiliates stood in a tight knit group, just in case any problem occurred. "One can never be to sure about opposition, drama could happen anytime; especially when the lines have been drawn. Who knows what those curry goat eating boomba clots are thinking." Divine told Jasheem and Freedom before leaving to go to the funeral.

When the ceremony ended, the whole crew hugged one another, exchanging fists and pounds. As they were dispersing, someone in the group could be heard saying, "Now, it's on for real. MPR for life!" In reply to this gesture about thirty or so youths joined in, shouting, "MPR!"

The scene looked like a morale ceremony in the army. Older people looked at the youths with question and concern. But after what happened to Little Daz, no one looked down on them. Everyone in his or her own way wanted justice. Some wanted revenge, while others wanted it to rest in the hands of the law or the lord above. It was one of those moments where everyone sincerely sympathized with the group because they were filled with anger themselves.

For the most part, everything went along smoothly at the funeral and for the first couple of days after, things were even quiet on the streets "Let them Jamaican mother fuckers sleep and think that we're pussy." Freedom said to Divine, because Divine wanted to retaliate right away, the same night of the funeral. Jasheem and Freedom were against the idea all together. Since Jasheem was from Brooklyn, he bumped heads with a lot of thugs from out that way. Therefore, he felt it was best they hired some gunslingers from East New York, otherwise known as the "Land of the

Coffins," for its notorious reputation throughout NYC for having the most ruthless hoods. The murder rate in this area verified this.

It was an easy situation to set up. All Jasheem did was make one phone call to his man Born Supreme, who also happened to be the leader of this squad out there called the Brooklyn Violators. The Brooklyn Violators were into robberies, extortion, and doing hits. Their reputation for busting their guns was well known, and when Jasheem presented the opportunity for the squad to take care of some contracts, they were more than happy to take care of things for MPR. These cats strived on drama. Money and problems went hand in hand as far as they were concerned. The strong survive and take, and the weak die and get taken from.

Three nights after the funeral, the Root posse gathered up to celebrate their victory. It was time to celebrate. A party was taking place at a little hole in the wall spot they frequented called The Diamond. As dance hall music played in the background, the scene was filled with ganja and plenty of dancing. Girls wore tight fitting dresses and skirts showing off plenty of their belongings.

When one walked in the spot the first thing they smelled was marijuana and the scent of vagina. The lights were dimmed very low, so along with the bumping and grinding, sex took place in a rhythmic dance like motion in the corners of the establishment and on the small, cramped dance floor. Yes! A party was going on, and the Root members felt they had plenty of reasons to celebrate.

In one corner of the small, poorly lit place sat a horse-shaped table with a couch extended around it. This spot was specifically designated for "Root" members. Ninja, Gunner, and Trouble, all teary eyed from smoking ganja and drinking, sat around in slump-like positions, laughing and joking amongst themselves as they watched their comrade Bullet get his dick sucked at the table by this freak he had just met on the dance floor.

"Stah, tell dah girl tah hit dah man off." Trouble jokingly said. They all started laughing; even Bullet chuckled a bit before catching himself. The hell with what they were talking about he thought, at least he was getting off, while they wished they were.

In another corner of the smoke den, Rasta Man sat at the bar drinking shots of Jamaican vodka and orange juice as he argued with his girlfriend, Crystal. Usually, she would not be caught dead in such a place as this because she hated his Root comrades and she hated the place because they frequented it and she couldn't trust him to go out on his own without messing with some man-stealing whore, as she called them.

"I want to go home!" she yelled out.

"Okay, okay, girl, in fifteen blood clot minutes we go."

For the most part, after Little Daz was killed, the streets remained scarily empty once the sun departed. This night was a little different because of the victory party taking place, so up until about twelve that night; "Root" members could be seen parading up and down the strip boasting arrogantly.

At about one in the morning, a tall West Indian cat came all the way from Brooklyn to join in the celebration. Before arriving, he was informed that the party at the nightspot was reserved for "Root" members and affiliates only. He wanted to celebrate badly, so he decided he'd have to lay his mack game down and scoop up one of the broads in the area who were known to the posse. It was just his luck because as he parked his car around the corner from the spot and got out, a group of ladies walked by and strolled into the neighborhood deli. They were dressed in a way that let him know they were from the Caribbean. They wore short, brightly colored, tight-fitting dresses, and lots of gold, which complemented their dark-complexioned bodies.

Walking behind the ladies into the store, the tall, well dressed, bronze-complexioned man took close inventory of himself. Feeling satisfied, he smiled, knowing that everything was all in his hands now. "Let the game begin," he whispered, speaking to no one in particular.

As he entered the store, all four ladies were standing near the freezer with their backs facing him, looking for refreshment drinks. As he approached the area, he too, pretended as if he was looking for a drink. They immediately noticed him and smiles spread across all of their faces; they made it no secret that they were taking notice of him. One of the ladies even went as far as to say, "Hey, good looking."

He smiled, knowing that he was in now and it was now all up to him to play his cards right. Turning toward her so that she could fully take notice of his good-looking features, he said shyly, "Hi, princess. How are you and your friends doing tonight?" She was mesmerized by his good looks and warm personality to the point where she could not respond. All she could do was join in with her friends as they laughed and giggled like shy teenagers. He was a master at taking females off their guard, so this situation was nothing to new to him. "It's on!" he thought to himself before continuing to lay his game down.

"I heard there's a party tonight. Are y'all ladies going?" waking up out of her daze, right away the young lady he called princess said in her cute West Indian accent,

"Dhats where we are bout to go. Do yah want tah go?" she asked, without any hesitation.

A victory smile spread wide across his face as he replied in his own little accent "Yeah, I would like dhat."

Without another word, he followed the ladies up to the counter without even bothering to grab anything for himself. As he paid for all of their items, the young lady asked, "What's yah name handsome?"

Without skipping a beat he turned towards her saying "Victorious."

This response caused her to blush and think, "Does he always win?"

Once outside with the young ladies, Victorious followed in step with the young lady on the side of him. Looking at his watch, he saw that it was now two in the morning.

Entering the front door of the club, one of the young ladies told the bouncer "Dhere wit me shakha."

Looking at Victorious up and down before moving out the way, he opened the door, but at the same time, the bouncer still kept an eye on the tall, unfamiliar guy in front of him. Not wanting to look suspicious and out of place, Victorious grabbed hold of the young lady's hand beside him and walked into the spot. Clouds of smoke surrounded them as they walked onto the dance floor and separated.

"Hold 'em down," one of her friends stated to her as she giggled.

The lady smiled back at her friends, grabbed his hand, and walked him onto the dance floor. Immediately, she started to grind and sway to the music as she rubbed against him. Although the freaky dance turned him on, his mind was strictly on what he came to do. Scanning the small establishment as they danced, he caught sight of his mark, who was sitting at the bar talking to a fine women sitting to the right of him.

"I can't lose sight of him," he told himself. By this time, he had found out practically everything about the young lady grinding on him except the color of her pubic hair. Her name was Roxy, and as it turned out Rasta Man, the guy he was watching, was her cousin. This he learned as they were sitting at the table drinking Guinness Stout. He wanted to get a close up look at the guy everyone called Rasta Man, so he told her that he was gonna get a bottle of stout from the bar. She didn't mind because by this time, she was intoxicated out of her mind and barely conscious. Victorious realized this right away, so he knew there was no need for him to rush to come back right away.

Approaching the bar, Victorious asked the bartender for another bottle of Guinness Stout. At the same time, he couldn't help but to hear the argument that Rasta Man and the lady next to him were having. From the looks of it, he figured the woman had to be his girlfriend because the argument was about him going home. Not to look suspicious, Victorious just sat there drinking the stout as he eavesdropped on their conversation.

Finally, at about 3:15, Rasta Man got up with the pretty lady storming behind. As he was leaving, he shook hands with almost everyone he passed. One could tell he was an important person among the group of peers by the way everyone approached him. Before walking out of the door, he and Shakha exchanged words, until his lady broke up the conversation, practically shoving him out the door and almost causing him to trip over his own feet. Waiting for about a minute to pass, Victorious followed suit. The feeling of butterflies began to fill his stomach as he thought about the situation at hand and passed Shakha on the way out. By this time, Shakha was even drunk, and did not even take notice of the man walking past him. Victorious felt relieved because this meant one less obstacle to deal with.

Victorious already knew what type of vehicle Rasta Man drove, where he would be parked at, and the best place to make the hit at. Feeling for the .38 revolver, which was tucked away inside the waistline of the back of his trousers, a rush of adrenaline shot through him; causing a sweat to break out in trickles on his forehead as he walked to the corner and awaited the arrival of what was to be.

The streets were completely empty of people; only streetlights and darkness existed, except for the occasional cars that would zoom by every now and then. The Roots celebration was about to come to an end abruptly at 3:30 on a Saturday morning.

Even as Rasta Man and his girlfriend Crystal approached his Range Rover, they continued to argue. This time, the argument was over who was driving home. Cyrstal kept telling him that he was too drunk to drive. But he insisted, "Fuck dhat I'm driving." It seemed like he was determined to not let her win. Stepping into the driver's side of the car, he revved up the vehicle, pulling out the parking lot not a second after she got in.

Seeing the headlights of the truck approaching as he stood at the corner, Victorious' first intention was to open fire on the vehicle as it got near. But then his decision changed when he saw the light was turning red.

Neither Rasta Man nor Crystal noticed the figure standing at the corner with a nickel-plated .38 revolver at his right side. The only thing they were aware of at the moment, were their own screams at one another as they continued to argue while coming to a stop at the red light. Rasta Man's words were cut off as two slugs crashed through the windshield directly in front of him. Victorious stood at the front of the bumper, before running over to the passenger's side, jumping onto the running board, and firing two shots through the window into Crystal, hitting her in the neck and head as she screamed for her dear life.

Feeling satisfied with the job, Victorious looked around to see if he could spot any visible witnesses. There was no one, he convinced himself. Acknowledging this, he placed the .38 back in the waist of his trousers and walked off around the corner toward his car. Cranking up the engine, he decided to head back to Brooklyn. Too bad, he thought to himself, he could not have spent the night with that pretty young lady back at the spot. Laughing, he remembered that she was Rasta Man's cousin. Luckily, he did not have to kill her as well. He sneered as he nodded his chin up and down.

"Fuck it," he told himself, sex is an every night opportunity when you're living the life and getting money.

The ironic thing was that as Victorious thought about having sex, the Roots lieutenant who they called Soldier was at home in bed with his wife having sex as someone crept through a living room window and walked into the bedroom, shooting him five times, without even as much as pointing the gun at his wife, who was now so filled with fright that she did not dare scream. The shadow just walked back to the living room and escaped out of the window from which it came.

The next day after roll call, Officer Frank told his partner Speedy, "What did I tell you? Didn't I tell you that there was gonna be a fucking mess to clean up!"

Speedy looked at him blankly, and hoped he gave Frank the impression that he did not give two shits about what happened. Frank paid him no mind and continued, "Rasta Man was shot to death along with his girl as they stopped at a red light coming from a Roots victory celebration."

Shaking his head he continued, "So much for celebrations, huh? And his lieutenant was killed as while he was at home having sex with his wife. And she can't recall a damn thing."

Speedy found this amusing, and replied, "He probably still has a hard on in the freezer in the morgue."

Frank just shook his head, walking off toward the locker room. Speedy laughed, knowing his partner was a little annoyed by his comment. Why Frank gave a hoot about these Negroes was beyond him.

Chapter Eight

A month after his arrest, Blaze was released on $2500 bail, which was posted by Rachel. He left the courtroom with Attorney Raynes at his side, as he reached the parking lot, he quickly noticed Rachel. Their eyes locked on one another before he winked, and turned to his lawyer to shake hands and exchange small talk. Mr. Raynes advised Blaze to stay out of trouble while the case was still pending because if he didn't, it could mess up his chances of getting off.

Walking toward the car, he felt a sense of happiness and smiled all the way into Rachel's arms. She was now standing at the hood of the car waiting. Embracing her, he lifted her small frame off the ground and told her, "You know I missed my baby, right?" Even though this was a statement more than anything else, he looked her in the face as if waiting on a reply. In return, she smiled as she laughed at his playfulness.

"You better because I missed you too. Your mom is mad that you decided to move in with me. But it's all good, because I'm a take care of you."

Placing Rachel back down on her feet, Blaze playfully palmed her buttocks with both of his hands squeezing. She liked this and squirmed and giggled at every touch. The both of them were so happy they were totally oblivious to the fact that they were now standing outside in public. Finally coming to his senses, Blaze hugged her hard, embracing her small frame one good time before smacking her again on her butt and walking to the passenger side and getting in the car.

It was a typical fall day and as Rachel drove, Blaze looked out at the leaves that covered the surrounding lawns and sidewalks like a blanket. The trees were empty and bare like the ones you would see in a horror flick. Blaze was mesmerized and caught up by the changing of the season. To him it was beautiful, yet ugly at the same time. The mysterious way things blossomed and then disappeared throughout the days of the year fascinated him.

Every now and then, Rachel would take her eyes off the road to look at him. She wondered what he was thinking about, but at first, was not going to ask. But then, curiosity took over.

"Blaze, what's the matter?" she asked, looking at him with question written all over her face.

Taking a minute to reply, Blaze turned to her shaking his head from side to side "Nah, it ain't nothing, baby. It ain't nothing," he said. Rachel knew him long enough to know that there was something bothering him. Yet, she also knew that if he did not want her to find out, then she would not find out. Realizing this as she drove on, she decided not to question him any further because she knew his thoughts were on everything that happened in the past five weeks. They both dove into deep thought the rest of the way home.

*   *   *   *   *

Sergeant Detective Aldoe sat in his office behind his desk. He was speaking on the phone while detective Jackson lounged on a swivel chair waiting for his superior to hang up and give him the low down on the events so far. A minute later, the sergeant hung up and gave the younger detective a broad, sinister smile.

"It seems that our buddy Mr. Jermaine is gonna beat the cases against him after all. Somehow, his lawyer cleverly managed to lay the blame solely on his partners who were murdered in that police raid five weeks ago. And to make a long story short, our hero just posted bail."

Smiling, while at the same time shaking his head from side to side; Detective Jackson did not utter a word. Instead, he picked up his mug of coffee from the top of the desk and began to sip.

*   *   *   *   *

In a small neighborhood diner called The Luncheonette, two figures sat talking as they ate lunch. Both ate like they were in a rush, yet the two young men chatted and talked freely, as if they knew each other since childhood.

"Yo sun, that's fucked up what King did," the light skinned brother stated, while his caramel complexioned partner shook his head in disbelief.

In a whisper-like tone, he replied, "Yeah, that cat's a bitch. But I'm a handle that myself, that coward violated for-real! And he was Infinite's cousin, so we trusted him on the strength that he was family. Then he snakes us after all the shit we did for him. That nigger didn't contribute anything to what we're about. Yet, he's driving a thirty thousand dollar car and sporting crazy jewelry. That bitch never got pussy before we got on. We made the fool a ghetto superstar."

Taking in a deep breath as hatred covered his face, he continued, "And I'm a kill that bitch, God watch. But as for that other coward, y'all handle that the way y'all wanna handle it. I just want him to pay any way that it comes. We just can't let Inf, Kariem, and Takim's deaths go like that. In life, everyone has to answer for his or her actions, word!"

Not saying anything else, they just gave each other a pound and handshake mixed together before continuing to eat. At the moment, they both had a lot to think about. There was a lot at hand to care of. "I just got home, and I'm already in the mix of this shit." Then the words of his mother scolding him kicked in. "Man," he told himself.

The next two days went by so quick and rapid that to Blaze it seemed like he just spoke to Divine yesterday. For two days, he had stayed home and did the family thing with Rachel and she loved every bit of it, the sex, the attention and just the fact that he was home. She almost wished that he never would leave the confines of their home. Yet, she knew for his own peace, solitude, and completeness he had to go out and do his thing in order for him to be happy. He was a street soldier at the heart, and for her to try to change him, would mean she would be changing the very things she loved about him. But she also was aware that the very things that she loved about him could also, in the end, destroy what they had together. This scared her so.

It had to be about seven in the morning when Blaze awoke. Lifting his head to turn over and look at Rachel, he noticed that she was not in bed. He had a hard on that was so erect, the front of his boxers stretched forward about six inches, causing him a little pain as his manhood sought to penetrate through. Where the fuck was she, he wondered, but then he remembered that she left for work six thirty every morning, Monday through Friday. "Damn Rachel!" he mumbled to himself as he thought about how good it would have been to sex her out at that moment. A cold shower would have to do, he told himself.

About an hour later, Blaze sat in the living room watching the news, "Good Morning New York" was on channel five. As he watched situation after situation being broadcast by reporters, he thought to himself.

New York never sleeps. Motherfuckers have to eat. How can a place with so much wealth be filled with so much poverty? And then they wonder why there is so much crime. Shit, the poor have to do what they have to do to get their's. The rich aren't the only ones who have to eat.

Thinking this caused him to think about his own situation and circumstances. He grew up poor as a child, so he knew how it felt to be hungry. And as a young man, he learned that money meant the difference between those who ate and those who starved. He'd rather be in jail or dead than starve for anyone. This was verified by the outlaw life that he decided to live. His life, he felt, was like that of a black cowboy in the early frontier. It was all about survival tactics.

One story in particular came on that caught his attention. It had something to do with an armored truck robbery in mid-town Manhattan in which they claimed over a million dollars was taken along with one of the guards being murdered. Thinking this over in his mind, Blaze came to the conclusion that it had to have been an inside job. Laughing to himself and shaking his head he said out loud, "Blacks couldn't pull off half the crimes that whites do. But, yet when you look at the news you would think that blacks are the only criminals. What a fucking world!" He clicked the "off" button on the remote, and then threw it on the floor. He was disgusted and frustrated to the point where he felt like screaming. Better yet, he felt like just lashing out at the world. "Why does life have to be so fucked up?" he wondered. He couldn't see what a big deal life was anyway. What the hell could life really mean to a person who came from nothing and never really had anything? When you strive to get something, somebody is always striving to knock you down and take it from you. So what's the sense of having shit? They aren't going to let a cat obtain but so much legally anyway. "Fuck that," he said aloud. That's why he planned to get money anyway he could.

"I don't make the rules. I'm just a player in the game" he would always tell Rachel whenever she would complain about his philosophy of the world because she felt that as a black man, he had the same opportunities as a white man. Plus, his mother worked so hard to provide him with the opportunities that so many like him did not have. He was lucky she would always tell him.

"You ain't no black man, so what you know?" he would always ask her whenever they got in these heated debates. To make things worse, Blaze and Rachel's father held a strong dislike for one another, and it didn't help that her dad was a police officer. To rub it in, Blaze would always tell her "Fuck the police! And fuck your dad too. Instead of the rich doing what they wished they could do, the police do it for them, since most of them are white anyway. The few black fuckers they have are nothing but foot soldiers in a war against the poor and working class."

Whenever he would go on about this she would cry because deep down inside, she felt it was partly true. She witnessed with her own eyes a few incidents where the police were basically acting like fascists and abusing the law as if they didn't have to follow it themselves, but she hated when he brought this up. After all, she felt her father was a different than the rest of them.

Blaze's mind was cluttered up with all different thoughts. It was just one of those days a black man goes through. He was confused, but at the same time, did not know what he was confused about. It all started off with him waking up in the morning not being able to look into Rachel's loving eyes. Not to mention the fact that he was not able to satisfy his early morning hard on. Then, King was a forever-lingering figure who clouded his thoughts; that situation had to come to a close.

As a matter of fact, as he sat on the couch contemplating, feeling the world on his shoulders, an idea came to him. From the day his attorney revealed King's identity as one of the snitches, Blaze knew what had to be done. King had to be disposed of; it was just a question of how it was going to take place. The first part of planning to do a crime is to think about how you're going to get away with it. Freedom is always an ultimate goal.

Blaze knew that King had no idea that he was aware that he dropped a dime, so Blaze decided to give him a friendly call and rock him to sleep. Why blow up his spot and make it harder for Blaze to get to the worm, when he could invite King to his own death at Blaze's own will on his terms.

Staring at the clock on the wall, Blaze noticed that it was ten-thirty. Taking a minute to think, he remembered that King started classes at twelve. Therefore, he was sure that King was up by now to answer the phone.

King had just woke up, which was a regular routine due to the alarm clock on the night stand being set the night before every morning to go off at ten-thirty.

Wiping the mucus out of his eyes as he yawned, King stretched while turning over to throw the covers off him and thought about the day ahead. After contemplating for a few, he decided to rest for another fifteen minutes. At that moment, the phone started ringing. Looking at the phone without picking it up, he thought to himself, "Damn, I need to go back to sleep." But after the fourth ring, he decided the phone was just going to keep on ringing and annoying him until he answered it. Reaching over and picking up the receiver, he asked, "Hello, who is this?"

For a minute, Blaze choked up. He didn't want to give any hint to King whatsoever about what his attentions were. So he held his composure the best he could and talked as smoothly as possible. For a second, he smiled as he thought about the game he was about to lay down on King.

"Yo, King what's the deal? This is Blaze."

King was stunned to hear Blaze's voice on the other end, and for a minute, he choked up as well. After a second or two, he regained his composure. Plus, why should he be shaken up if Blaze didn't know what happened?

"Oh! Blaze, what's the deal yo?" then he continued, "I heard you had just got out." This was lie because for all he knew, Blaze was going down for a long time. "When are we gonna chill, god?" he asked. King figured Blaze would pass up the opportunity since he was a square and not the type of cat Blaze kept in company with.

To his surprise, Blaze replied, "King, that's what I was thinking about. That shit that happened to Infinite was kind of fucked up. And I know that it hit you hard. I know that we were never close, but you're family, Inf was my peoples. And he was your cousin, so you know we have to keep shit tight even though he's gone. Maybe we can get up tonight, and go have some drinks and fuck with some freaks. I'll meet you at your house at nine."

Blaze knew it was ok with King. King wished from day one that he could be down with the program, and kind of always looked up to Blaze and Infinite. He was in their shadows, so Blaze knew that whatever he asked of the man, at the moment, he would do. Especially if he had any remorse about what happened to Inf.

"Yeah, god come by my crib at nine. I need to get out and get my freak on anyway, word! So I'll see you then." With that said, they both hung up. He really didn't want to talk any longer, and for a minute wished he did not pick the phone up. Contemplating this for a little while, King decided that it couldn't hurt any to hang out with the man for a couple of hours.

At the moment, he had other things to worry about, like taking a shower and getting ready for class. As it was, he was running late and behind schedule, so with no delay, he began doing what he had to do.

Blaze, on the other hand, hung up the phone and could not get his mind off the situation at all. To him, it seemed like there was just not enough time to prepare for the day ahead.

For a minute, he really thought about scratching the idea out of his mind all together. But as he thought about his dead friend, he knew King had to pay for his actions, and it would not feel the same if someone else took care of it. This was personal vengeance.

The following eight hours went by so quickly for the both of them that it was like going to sleep one minute and then waking up the next. Blaze was kind of nervous and anxious to get it on. While King, on the other hand, had no clue whatsoever about what was gonna go down. His mind was strictly on partying and sex. He knew with Blaze's reputation and presence, any club they entered would be like a regular stomping ground to the ghetto superstar. Other cats would player hate, while their broads would do anything to get his attention.

At about a quarter to nine, as King just finished dressing, Blaze pulled up into the driveway, pimping an up-to-date model Nissan Pathfinder jeep. King knew it was him once he heard the beeping of the horn coming from the driveway. Who else could it be he thought to himself? And as he ran from the bathroom to the front door to look out through the small windows situated along the top of the door, he could see Blaze rocking back and forth to the music. "Don't believe the hype!" by Public Enemy was playing and he could feel the base vibrating through the air. After pointing to Blaze so he would notice that he was aware of his arrival he ran to get the Tommy Hilfiger spring jacket that he left laying on the bed.

Once inside the jeep King and Blaze gave each other pounds. The music was playing so loud, so neither of them spoke. That's the way Blaze wanted it, he had to calm his nerves so he would not shoot the rat bastard as they drove.

As they rode, a sense of calmness came over Blaze. There was no need to panic or over think things now. He knew what he had to do; while at the same time acknowledging what was at stake if he made any mistake "There's no room for mistakes." he always told himself whenever he was doing something criminal. That's the reality when your freedom is the price to pay.

Coming to a stop sign he turned down the music, while he looked at King. As he stared at him, he felt a sense of pity for the kid. Even though they were both around the same age, it was like they came from two different worlds. Both came from solid homes, yet both had decided to venture off into the criminal world. One embraced the code of the streets, while the other was scared to face the music once presented with the reality of the tune. Why is it that some people fail to realize that there is a price to pay for everything? Even as a child one comes to realize that one day we are all going to die. Why did this cat think that he could reap the awards that crime pays, yet not hold his water when the long arm of the law reached out to him? He was a soldier in this war, but he failed to put on his uniform. Because of this, some of his brothers died while many others were captured and arrested. For this, he was going to pay.

Shutting off the music Blaze said, "Yo, sun, we're going to this club called 27A on Main Street in Bayshore. That shit be jumping on Fridays. Word is bond! Mad cuties be up in there, plus my man and them are bouncers there, so we'll get in free. But first we have to pick up some product from one of the stash houses that was left after one of the raids."

Blaze had knowledge of all the drug spots the family utilized. Since many of the family members were now locked up, a lot of the houses were now without supervision. One of the spots was on Wicks road in Brentwood.

King didn't bother to say anything, he was thinking about partying and getting his shit off. As Blaze turned the music back on, King dozed off into a comfortable sleep.

It was about a half an hour ride before Blaze pulled onto a block, which was a block away from the house. Camouflaging the truck, he pulled up alongside the woods across the street.

Noticing that King was still fast asleep, Blaze reached into his Nautica spring coat, pulled out leather gloves and placed them on. As one hand turned the tape deck off, the other nudged at King, awakening him.

"Yo, god, we're here" Blaze told him as he jumped out the driver side not giving King anytime to respond.

King was awake but all his senses were not quite there yet. Yawning and wiping his eyes, he stepped out the passenger side, closing the door lightly. Since the doors had magnets, it shut closed without making much of a noise at all.

Now standing outside of the truck, King looked around the unfamiliar surroundings. He wasn't scared; he just wondered where they were. Blaze noticed King's bewilderment as he came from the back of the truck with a flashlight.

"Yo, sun, I parked over here cuz, I don't want anyone to see us going inside the crib." Pointing to an opening about four or five feet wide he said, "This path leads to the backyard." Without saying anything else, he began to walk through the opening.

King looked around at first before deciding to follow Blaze's footsteps into the path surrounded by trees and darkness. As he followed, he could see the house in the distance. Blaze jumped over the fence and stood the other side waiting on him. Leaping over the fence, using both hands to support himself by holding the top rail, King followed suit. The foundation rattled as the fence made a "click, click," sound. Hitting the ground with both feet, he followed Blaze, who was now heading toward the back door of the house.

As Blaze reached the steps, he ducked down, extending his right hand into the surrounding bushes, coming out with a set of keys. Two keys dangled from the key ring. As he stood, he automatically guessed that one was for the back door and the other was to the front.

Fitting one of the keys into the back door, on the first turn around it clicked open. He turned to King and smiled, saying, "Come on, god, let's go get this shit and get out of here quickly!"

Once Blaze was inside the house and the door was closed with King behind him Blaze mentioned, "The products in the basement."

The flashlight beamed, giving them sight as to what direction to take. Blaze found the basement door. He turned the knob and slowly opened the door, revealing steps going downward.

Butterflies started to enter Blaze's stomach all at once, as he thought about what was going to take place. Now, all he could think about was pulling the job off without any unnecessary problems.

Walking down the steps, Blaze did not need to look to see if King was behind him. With all the darkness that surrounded them he knew King would follow willingly; especially since Blaze held the flashlight, which was the only source of light.

Reaching the bottom of the steps, Blaze thought about how he could hear King's breathing, along with the rhythm of his own heart beating. Entering one of the bedrooms, Blaze called out to King.

"Yo, god, come over here."

As soon as King entered the bedroom, the door slammed shut behind him, making a loud noise, which seemed to echo forever. A bright light zeroed in on King's face. Blaze stood before him, calm, but with a crazed look. The flashlight was in his right hand, but King also noticed immediately what looked to be a chrome .38 caliber snub nose in his left. The gun was pointed directly at his chest.

King didn't know what to do, whether to be scared for his life or to take it as a joke and laugh. But as he stared steadily into Blazes eyes, he saw fury in them that he never saw before in another man. His stomach ached and a flash of heat shot through him causing his bowels to want to release.

Staring into King's eyes, Blaze manifested a half grin, not showing one tooth in the process. He truly disliked this man in front of him for all the trouble he caused and thought about just shooting him and getting it over right away in a one-two-three fashion. Instead, he decided he was going to let King know the reason why he was going to meet his maker. Blaze wanted him to leave this earth with a guilty conscious.

"King, you know why this happening to you, right? Well, if you don't know why, then I'm a tell you. Your loose lips damn near got the whole family murdered and those who didn't get their wigs pushed back got locked up." Pausing for a second to look at the horror in King's face he went on. "Fuck everybody else, including me. But how could you do it to your own cousin?"

Pistol-whipping him to the ground, he asked again, "You little faggot, how could you do it to your cousin?"

King was positioned in a stance half way on his knees, damn near crouched against the wall. He was scared beyond any point he had ever been in his life. His fear outweighed the pain as Blaze kept butting him in the head with gun. He tried to block each blow, but at the same time, was scared that Blaze would shoot, so he did not try jumping at the man and wrestling the gun away. Saliva mixed with blood spilled in streams as he choked and spit. Gashes opened in his face and forehead revealing flesh as Blaze went into a blind fury, oblivious to King's yells and pleas for him to stop. King balled into a fetal position, seeking to cover his face from the blows.

Blaze was frustrated beyond imagination and too far gone to stop now. The more he beat King and heard his whimpers, the more satisfied he became and the more he lusted for King to feel the judgment for his actions.

Backing up a few steps from King while still shining the flashlight on his face, Blaze took careful aim and stood there for 10 seconds.

King screamed "No!" but this was his last yell before two shots were released into his bloodied face, shattering his cheekbone, slamming his head against the wall. As his body slumped to the floor, crimson red bloodstains remained on the white sheetrock wall.

Seeing the lifeless body woke Blaze out of his fury, leaving his mind with one thought: to get the hell out of there as quickly as possible. His mind was blank but his body was moving. He ran up the stairs and out the back door, closing it behind him. Taking large strides down the stairs, he ran into the backyard, leaping over the fence and dashing through the path towards the jeep.

Once inside his truck he placed both the flashlight and gun on the passenger side of the seat. He really could not recall how he made it this far. His body felt completely drained and he wanted to vomit badly. "Fight back the urge," he told himself, placing the key into the ignition, pulling off slowly down the street, while looking around to make sure no one was watching. He turned on the headlights once he was about three blocks away.

Coming to his senses about a quarter a mile away, he realized he needed to get rid of the gun and get cleaned up right away. Dipping from lane to lane, he moved the large truck in traffic at normal speed. Now that he was calm and able to think, he decided he'd stop somewhere on Sunrise Highway, bury the evidence in the woods, and change.

Taking inventory of himself, he felt cool from all the sweat, which soaked his clothing and clung to his body. "In all my workouts back in school on the wrestling team, I never sweated so much." he said to himself.

"Wooh, I almost lost it," he whispered. "This is getting crazy!" He started inhaling and exhaling in deep breaths. He felt no remorse about what was done, and in a way it bothered him.

It was amazing that on this Friday night there were hardly any patrol cars out on the highway. This is one of the first things Blaze took notice of as he headed out east. Usually patrol cars would be all along the highway and parked in camouflage as they hid from oncoming traffic behind bridges and on the grass.

Looking up at the sign which read, Exit 64 Bellport Station Road, Blaze knew once he passed the exit, there would be a long stretch of woods just beyond. Knowing the area well, he also knew it was safe to park alongside the highway and discard of the gun and clothing because the area was extremely dark and secluded.

Pulling up into a stretch of woods just beyond the exit, Blaze looked in the rearview mirror to see if he could see anyone on the adjoining service road. Seeing that it looked pretty safe, he decided he had found the perfect spot.

Taking in a deep breath and exhaling, he brought the jeep to a stop before once again looking in the rearview mirror at the passing traffic. "No need to be paranoid now," he whispered to himself. Grabbing the flashlight, a bag containing a new outfit that Rachel had bought him earlier, and the .38, he stepped out of the vehicle in a rush, knowing there was not a second to waste. He realized that the quicker he took care of business the safer he would be. Acknowledging this fact gave him comfort because no one knew about what happened but him and he sure as hell was not going to tell on himself.

Blaze did not turn on the flashlight until he reached the foot of the woods. As he entered the brush, a gush of wind shot past him. It was kind of chilly and he shivered a little as he thought about it. After walking about 100 feet in, he squatted down on both knees and began digging with the butt of the revolver and his gloved hands. All he needed was a hole about two feet deep he told himself.

Once the hole was dug out, Blaze felt satisfied with himself and without hesitating, he threw the gun down and began to cover the hole with earth and leaves. Undressing, he quickly discarded the sweaty, blood-stained garments by creating and then burying them in another hole. This time he dug a hole about three feet deep.

Creeping out of the brush, Blaze looked around to make sure there was no one around before running towards the jeep, jumping behind wheel, and pulling off into oncoming traffic slowly.

His whole state of mind and presence felt lighter and stress-free at that moment. He didn't have a worry in the world besides his conscious, which was not really bothering him. He did what he felt was necessary to do. So he had no reason to be bothered, he reasoned, after thinking about it for a moment. His mother's whispers about values and being a good person were the only echoes, which haunted him at the moment. He realized that no matter what the reason, taking another man's life was beyond justification, especially another black man's life. He swore his mother would disown him and curse all the prophets if she knew what he had done. She would never find out either, he would go to his grave with this secret, to protect himself and her sanity.

His mother would never understand why he chose this life over the protective shield she had struggled all her life to build for him, to graduate school go onto college and then get a good job. To be involved within the life of crime is to be a citizen of another world within the world that one lives in. The codes and the laws of the streets are not flexible like the court system. In the streets, there's a thin line between life and death. It just so happens that because of the ever-present poverty in the ghettos, the children born into these surroundings usually are the ones who are the easiest to lure into such a life. Not everyone is going to obtain the American dream of a college degree, and a big house with a picketed fence. Some are going to die, or spend their lives in jail. Yes, he could have chosen a different path because of the opportunities his mother provided, but this was his life and his choice, and he was set on living it the way he wanted to with no remorse for the time being. Maybe things would change later. But for now he was playing by the rules.

*   *   *   *   *

It's been about ten months since Blaze's release from prison and seven since King's body was found. King got a two-paragraph article dedicated to him in the local paper. In so many words, it stated that he was a college student with no previous criminal record. No big deal, in other words, just another nigger dead. The article was so small that Blaze wondered why they even bothered to print anything at all.

Blaze sat back in his favorite recliner pondering all the events that had taken place since his release. Except for King's situation, business could have never been better. His personal life, on the other hand, was another matter all together. He and Rachel were no longer together because she claimed she claimed he was becoming more distant by the day and she couldn't take his behavior anymore. She told him that he had a wish for his own death; and that she would rather not be with him when it happened because it would be partly her fault if she just sat there and acted like she didn't see the writing on the wall.

"You and that superstitious shit he would always tell her."

One night, Blaze came storming into the house like a madman. Rachel was sitting in the living room watching TV and at first did not notice that he passed her. But after hearing the kitchen water running and the noise he was making pushing dishes and utensils aside, she looked up toward the hallway which led to the kitchen. Her first instincts were to scream, but then she decided against the idea, and instead chose to run to his aid.

What first caught her attention were the trickles of blood that she saw on the living room carpet leading into the kitchen's tiled floor.

Rachel's heart was pounding unusually fast, to the point where she could hear what was going on inside her. She was thinking the worst, and as she ran into the kitchen, what she saw almost confirmed what she was thinking. Her mind snapped before she could think and she screamed "Oh my God!"

Blaze stood in front of the kitchen sink with his shirt torn and falling to his waistline. He breathed heavily. Blood drops were all over the floor and smeared on his body and clothing. The sink was layered with a cherry Kool-Aid looking substance. At first glance, it looked like he was shot. But as he stood there wiping himself with a rag, Rachel came in screaming "Oh my god!"

He told her, "Calm down! Calm down, I'm not shot! These cats tried to jump me and I shot one of them."

He was lying of course, and as he told her the lie he never once looked her in the face, instead, he kept his eyes fixed on the rag he was using to cleanse himself. He was not even aware she had walked off and retreated to the bedroom in tears to pack her stuff.

Rachel packed her clothes in bags, screaming and crying.

"I can't take it any more, I can't take it no more! One of these days I'm going to be identifying your body!"

At this point, she knew she had seen enough and had to escape the situation while she had the chance. She loved him too much to be around and see him destroy his life. Running like someone was chasing her she went downstairs to the room and started packing.

He tried to stop her as she dragged her bags across the floor through the front door, but she would not hear a word he had to say, and left without saying one word. Her tears said it all, telling her heart's desires and pain without words.

Tears streamed down Blaze's cheeks as he thought about the good times he and Rachel had together. He really did miss her. Around her, he could be a real person and show his true feelings. He could lean on her just as well as she could lean on him. Yet, he knew that her departure was the best thing for the both of them. He was a part of something that she could never understand. And he was evolving into something that even he did not quite understand. At times, he didn't even understand the life he lived. All he knew was that he was alive, and as long as he was alive he was going to get his and do what was necessary to insure that he stayed on top and alive. To him, his world and reality was just a smaller reflection of what went on in the upper levels of society. "I have to eat just like rich people," was his motto.

Wiping away the moisture from his face, Blaze thought about what was to come. There was one more situation from the past to take care of. Picking up his cell phone, he began dialing. After waiting for the number to go through and hearing three beeps, he then dialed his number followed by the star button, and then 911 as the code.

Blaze walked into the kitchen to get a glass of orange juice and it wasn't even a minute before his phone began to ring. Picking up the receiver on the wall, he hoped that it was whomever he paged calling because right then, he was not in the mood for small talk.

"Who's speaking?" he asked in a kind of irritated tone of voice.

"What's the deal, god? I seen your number on my pager." The person on the other end replied.

"Yo, god, I been thinking about that situation that I wanted you to handle. I want you to take care of that. Right now is about the time for that to go down. Word is bond!" Blaze answered as if he was even trying to convince himself about the situation.

"Alright, gee, there's no more to be said. It'll be taken care of A.S.A.P., I'll give you a call when it's all handled. Peace!" he stated before hanging up.

Blaze was feeling kind of edgy. But at the same time, he had confidence in the man on the end of the other line. He kept it real up to this point, so why should he sham on him now, Blaze told himself.

Meanwhile, the man on the other end of the line hung up and called someone else after he finished talking to Blaze. After exchanging small talk for about three minutes, the other person on the line guaranteed that the situation would be taken care of before the end of the night, at which time, he would call to verify that all was well and to set up a meeting place to collect his pay.

As this individual hung up the phone, he walked into one of the back rooms. Once he opened the closet door, a safe stood in plain view. After spinning the dial three times to the right, two times to the left, and once to the right again, he heard a clicking sound. Pulling the handle-like lever, he opened the swinging door, which revealed nothing but semi-automatic weapons. He already knew what he wanted, so without hesitating, he grabbed his chrome 357.

Placing the gun in his pants at the waistline, he thought about what was going to take place. He wasn't a bit fazed at all; in fact, to him, it was just going to be another situation to take place in the ever-changing world in which he lived. Plus the pay-off was going to be real nice. This was all he really cared about. He was a snake to his heart. He'd even cross himself if the money was right. Thinking about this caused him to let out a series of chuckles.

Looking at his watch he noticed that it was six' clock, he knew just how much time he had to spare before everything had to go down. It was all in his hands now that the green light was given. No one but God and himself, could alter this plan.

It was drizzling on and off. Nothing major, but still enough rain to keep anyone from standing outside for a long time without an umbrella. It was Friday, so even though the weather was not wonderful, a steady flow of cars kept pulling up to the house. This was a crack spot, so cars pulled up and pulled one after another continuously.

Two youths in their early teens, geared in Columbia sweat suits and Timberlands took turns serving the customers. As they received the money, they would stuff the bills inside their pants pockets, which were bulging since they had been on shift for over two hours.

Inside the house, Steve sat at a rectangular table doing the books for the day, like he did every night at about this time. But because it was Friday, he also had to tally the week's earnings so the boss could come by later that night to collect the day's earnings and take notes on the week's earnings.

As the hours passed by, Steve became overly anxious to the point where he was almost fidgeting. On top of being anxious, he was also a little nervous about the hour ahead.

When 9'0clock touched down, he told his two shorties to close down shop and get ready to bounce. By 9 PM, they were paid their weekly salary of five hundred, and on their way. Needless to say, they were more than happy to get off an hour early, so happy that they said not one word to Steve as he handed them the envelopes.

Once they got up out of there, Steve locked up the door and lied down on the couch. He was hoping to be able to catch some zzz's before the boss showed up. "Beep, beep," the sound of a car's horn awoke him. Knowing whom it was already; he jumped up grabbing the black plastic bag containing the scales and account book and bounced out the back door. As he approached the Mercedes utility truck, he handed the plastic bag to Boom.

"What's up?" Boom asked.

"The regular," replied Steve as he got in on the passenger side. Leaning back in the seat, he gave Boom a pound as he told him, "Stop by a phone, cuz I gotta make a call."

Looking at him a little confused and dumbfounded Boom told him "Yo, use my car phone."

Steve smirked replying "Nah, I gotta call a customer. I can't use your phone cuz you never know if their phone's tapped. Plus, the police be intercepting them cell phone calls."

Not wanting to argue the point, Boom replied, "Okay, I'll stop at the gas station."

On the way to the gas station, Steve stayed unusually quiet. His mind was on what was going to take place in a few minutes. As they pulled up next to one of the pumps at the gas station, Steve jumped out, practically sprinting to the phone.

In the same town, a mile away in a motel room three individuals waited, two males and one female. Patiently, they awaited that one important phone call. Each of them wore black from head to toe. A duffel bag containing two nines and a mini 22 caliber Uzi with a 100 round banana clip, sat at the foot of the bed.

The phone rang once and then on the second ring the female picked up. They were stationed in that room since twelve in the morning, so this was the moment they were waiting for. Everything was set up precise and to the point. So it was already planned for the lady to pick up the phone.

"Ready," she said, which was the code word.

"Mercedes truck" Steve replied and hung up. Butterflies along with a slight headache crept up on him as he walked back to the truck. Once he got in, he told Boom "Let's stop at McDonald's before you drop me off."

Hanging up the phone the blonde haired woman gave her two male partners a thumb up sign. Seeing this, one of the guys grabbed the duffel bag and walked out the door, leaving them to follow. Sitting inside the van, all three of them chose their weapon before the van was even started. Once this was done the woman started the van and pulled off, skidding a little, and accelerating to 80mph in seconds. It was now time to rock and roll. The destination as to where Boom and Steve were going was already planned. Their only job was to get there and handle business.

Pulling out of the gas station parking lot, skidding as the tires hit a patch of gravel, Boom accelerated the Benz truck down the block toward King Kullen shopping center where McDonalds was located. Skirting into the parking lot, Steve could see that there were only about five cars inside, and all of the occupants were inside the store. He was nervous at this point, and hoped that nothing went wrong. Beads of sweat started to form along his forehead as he sat back as stiff as a dead man. Even Boom noticed that something was wrong with his cousin, and for a minute was concerned that Steve was sick or something.

As he parked and turned the car ignition off he asked, "What's the deal, sun? You alright?"

Steve quickly woke up out of his daze saying, "Yeah, yeah, I'm alright, bee."

In unison, they both stepped out of the truck, slamming the doors behind them as they walked off. Although the day had been for the most part wet and dreary, the night's sky was clear and beautiful. Boom noticed how beautiful it looked and how fresh the air smelled, right away. He really regretted having to walk into the fast food joint to order because the air was so refreshing outside.

At the counter there only stood one patron on line, who was taken care of in a matter of minutes. A young lady, who looked no more than seventeen years old, stepped up to the register smiling.

"Welcome to McDonald's can I help you with your order?'

Immediately, Boom who towered over the young lady ordered.

"Let me get two Big Mac's, a super-size order of fries, and a vanilla shake."

As she rung this up, she looked at Steve and asked, "Are y'all ordering together?"

Steve nervously replied, "Yeah, can I have a fish fillet sandwich, super-size fries, and a large Sprite." Belching, he pounded on his chest, chuckling while Boom and the young lady looked at him, laughing in unison.

"Man, you need to take your nasty ass outta here," Boom stated, banging the counter with his left fist, crouching as he continued to laugh.

Under normal circumstances, Steve would have laughed, but he was still a little nervous. As it was, he knew that he was not going to be able to eat the food he ordered.

Boom handed the chuckling young lady a twenty, saying, "My apologies for this fool." Again, they both started laughing as she rung up the meal and handed him the change.

Stepping out of the exit doors with a bag in each of their hands, Steve walked three steps behind Boom. Coming within about seven feet of the front grill of the Mercedes truck, Boom dropped his bag as he strived to back up and run. "Steve they got guns!" he screamed, but Steve had already dodged behind another parked car.

A female figure, dressed all in black, stood swinging an Uzi from side to side. The bullets cut into Boom's back like darts, pounding into him while some ricocheted off the ground.

Boom lay sprawled out on his stomach as his blood poured aimlessly from out of the little holes in his body and onto the ground, forming a pool of crimson red life matter around his body. He died after the first five bullets hit him, the rest other fifteen or so were unnecessary.

Steve pretended to pull out the 357 as the two gunmen were on him in a matter of seconds, with guns outstretched to his head. One of them stepped behind him, pushing him to get inside the van, while the other kept his gun pointed directly at his cranium.

People screamed as they heard the initial bullets. After seeing a man rushed inside a van, the store's workers and patrons ran out to see to two bags of food and drinks sprawled all over the ground as blood mixed with Boom's milkshake, about two feet from where he lay lifeless.

Crowds of horrified onlookers surrounded Boom's remains, and within minutes, sirens could be heard in the distance. In about one minute, eight marked police cars pulled up with sirens flashing, and lights blazing. The officers jumped out, running to the scene.

In the back of the van, Steve sat with the two gunmen. Their guns were no longer drawn because that had all been a front for any would-be viewers or spectators. The fact was, Steve set his own cousin up to get murdered. His take was thirty-five thousand, ten of which, he was paid in advance, six months earlier.

Once the first officers arrived at Boom's body, they pushed everyone back. Some of the other officers questioned and jotted down the home addresses of possible witnesses on the scene. From what information they gathered, it seemed that two black males were ambushed while they walked out of the McDonald's establishment. One was murdered and the other was kidnapped. Seeing this, the sergeant in blue and white radioed in what they had, so the report could be issued to the captain.

Boom's body lay blanketed by a white sheet for about twenty minutes before an ambulance arrived to take him to the morgue. The attendants squirmed as they picked up his six-foot, bloodless life form, strapping it to the stretcher. "This guy must have been shot like thirty times!" one of the attendants mentioned, not speaking to anyone in particular. No one else said anything as they looked on in disbelief.

As the ambulance pulled away, the crime scene unit began to tape off the area and comb for bullet shell casings. Immediately as they began to do this, they ran everyone away from the area, even other police officers, who were always annoyed by the routine that these people pulled every time they arrived on a murder scene.

The rest of the night was strictly routine for the crime scene unit and detectives who were on the scene. . It was just another day on the job, nothing unusual or out of place; these types of crimes occurred on an every day basis.

Chapter Nine

In front of the mirror, she stood brushing her long, silky-textured, blonde hair. As the young lady in her early twenties looked into the six foot tall mirror, she observed every fine detail of her naked body, which caused her to begin breathing heavily. Dropping the brush to the floor with both hands, she gently began to caress both breasts slowly. Imagination took over her as she thought about the sex that was about to take place between her and Divine. Her crotch was swollen and pulsating as juices began to stream down in between the inner parts of her thighs. How she needed to get fucked badly, was all that was on her mind as she began to finger herself with one hand and rub her breasts with the other. The sight and participation in the night's violence turned her on immensely and awoke the desire for sex within her. And it was not ironic that she also enjoyed having rough, physical sex.

An hour had passed by since she had called Divine to fill him in on the night's happenings. He was pleased to say the least, and had promised to swing by her house within the next hour or two. She knew what this meant and was garbed in a black satin-laced two-piece pajama set. It was no coincidence either because, she knew that seeing her curved out frame turned him on. She was his weakness, a female gangster and a freak. Something he had not experienced with any other woman. She knew for sure that he was not dropping by and leaving without hitting her off once he set eyes upon her.

The temperature in the one bedroom condo was warm and very comfortable. Wall to wall carpet surrounded every aspect of the floors except for the tiled kitchen. As she walked from the bedroom to the living room, basically naked, she thought about how good the bottoms of her feet felt as she dragged them across the carpet.

Sitting down in her favorite chair, she sunk down within the soft surrounding leather as her hands rested on both leathered chair arms. Just as she started to sink deep in thought, the sound of the doorbell awoke her.

"Hold on," she screamed as she basically lunged herself out the chair, running toward the door.

"Hey, baby" she said, as a smile from ear to ear illuminated her tanned face.

He held out his arms to her and she leaped into them, practically smothering him as she planted wet kisses all over his face. The way she thirsted for him turned him on. He had loved other women, but he craved this woman.

Planting her on her feet with both hands positioned around her waist, he pecked her on her forehead, watching her squirm with delight to his every touch.

"How's my angel doing?" he asked with a straight face. He knew that calling her angel would get her open because it always got her going. She loved every bit of it, and he knew it too. He also realized that he had to keep it like that because she was so valuable to him, so he could not afford to have it any other way. She was his little soldier, and the fact that she was white, made it that much more wonderful and glamorous. Her skin tone allowed her to get in places that were impossible for him and his team to enter. Plus, she had more heart than plenty of the guys he knew. Boom was the third hit that she handled for the organization. Thinking about this brought him to the realization that it was best to keep her on his side. She was plain fire and emotion.

Sheena loved when Divine spent time with her, it made her feel special. She was all smiles when he inquired about how she was doing. Just having him there was enough for her. Looking at him for one second brought butterflies to her stomach. She loved him. Why else would she be doing the things that she did for him?

When Sheena came out of the army from being on active duty for four years, she decided that if she could kill for the government, protecting their interests and get paid practically nothing for it, then she could go into business for herself, take contracts, and really get paid for her services. Around this time, a childhood friend of hers, who was a member of the Brooklyn Violators, introduced her to Divine. The Brooklyn Violators was a crew that took jobs for MPR here and there.

Although the relationship that Sheena and Divine had was based on a need and demand situation, in due time, she came to love him even though he was her employer. The things he asked her to take care of became personal. And as far as she was concerned, whoever was his enemy was also hers.

Picking her up off her feet once again, he placed her on the bed with her buttocks positioned on the edge. At that moment, he placed his right pointer finger over his lips, signaling for her to be quiet. With this done, he began to kiss her ferociously, as her hands rubbed his chest up and down, side to side. Pushing her down on her back with both of her legs cocked up on both sides of him, he then began to kiss, nibble, and suck on her from her neck down to her crotch, which was still covered her bikini.

Stepping back two feet without saying anything, Divine began to undress until he was naked. Positioning himself to enter her, he then placed his hands in back of her to unfasten her bikini top. Once this was done he wasted no time placing himself inside of her, feeling the tight wetness envelop around his penis. As he grabbed hold of her ass, he entered with hard penetrating thrusts. She screamed and panted with pleasure, cheering him on.

"Fuck me harder!" she kept screaming through gasps of breath, as he pounded away, placing her legs up on both of his shoulder blades.

Turning her over on her knees, he entered her from the doggie style position until she told him to fuck her in the ass. "She's a freak to her heart," he thought to himself. But so was he, so without hesitation he complied, pulling her long hair as he did so.

The sex lasted for an hour and a half. And after it was all over, they both got up exhausted, practically pushing each other all the way to the shower.

He washed her as she washed him without conversation. As his manhood got hard once again, she went down on him, taking all nine inches into her mouth, causing him to close his eyes and moan with pleasure, as the water rained down on them both.

After coming out the shower and drying each other off, he told her, "I want you to have a rental car parked in my driveway, cuz I got something to take care of tomorrow night. So have it there by five, okay."

Sheena knew better than to him to ask him any questions. Besides, he was her employer, and she was just happy they had flexibility they in their unspoken agreement between one another.

So without hesitation, she replied, "Baby, I'll handle it for you by four tomorrow."

They spent the next hour hugged up together on the living room couch watching the news, until Divine decided to bounce. This was nothing unusual because they never spent the night together.

Once he was inside his car he made the call to his comrade. "The job was taken care of."

*   *   *   *   *

The next morning, there was a slight drizzle coming down. Tree branches swayed as a slight breeze blew, causing the drizzle to hit objects harder than it normally would. The sky was gray with clouds as if the sun did not exist at all.

Raindrops echoed against the house consistently, without skipping a beat. He could feel the dampness settling in his bones, giving him a chill as he sought to wrap the covers tighter around him. It had to be about seven-thirty in the morning he thought. Yet, it did not matter what time it was to him because all he wanted to do was rest. The man did not know whether it was the job or family life. But he did know that he was fatigued and stressed to the point where he felt like going to somewhere on this earth, where there was no civilization so he could be alone.

Being a father and a mentor; a husband and companion; a police officer and a mediator between God and the devil on the streets, was getting to be too much for him. The thought of it all made him want to cry. Placing both hands on his face, he began to shake his head from side to side and wonder.

"Ring, ring," the sound of the phone immediately awoke him out of his daze. Without even thinking, he automatically reached over and picked up the phone.

"Detective Aldoe, who's speaking?" he asked in a raspy morning voice. For a minute, the other person on the line said nothing. Just as he was about to hang up, the person on the other end answered.

"Before you hang up, detective, hear me out" Detective Aldoe seriously thought about hanging up on her, but then decided against it.

Instead, he asked, "What do you want Ms. Simmons?" wondering what game she was playing. Being the confident person she was, she went on without hesitation.

"Listen, detective, I know that we are not on the best of terms, but for professional purposes, let's put all that aside. We can serve each other better by dealing with one another than by acting like children and ignoring one another."

Before she could say anything else, he cut her off, "So, what do you have in mind?" he knew that there was something to this call besides a request for friendship. He just wanted to cut through all the bullshit and find out what her real objective was.

She, on the other hand, felt kind of bad about what took place between them and how it all ended. She truly wanted reconcile, and what better way to achieve this than by helping him with his job. So she answered "Well, I don't know whether you're aware or not, but the second informant on the big case that took place ten months ago involving the so called Brotherhood was murdered last

night in the parking lot of a McDonald's. A second victim who
was with him was possibly kidnapped. To make a long story short,
I thought that it just seemed like too much of a coincidence that
both informants were murdered after one of the main suspects,
Jermaine Jackson, whose nickname is Blaze, was released from
prison. If you ask me, it seems like your little syndicate is still in
operation."

Thinking to himself as she spoke, his brain started to race as he
recalled the events leading to the investigation. "You're probably
right," he stated, pausing for a moment before continuing. "But I
don't think he committed any of the murders himself. Yet, there is
a chance he may know what happened. We can't arrest him though
on suspicion, and what we have is pure accusations and
circumstantial. When he first came home we had him under
surveillance for two months. And boy, was he squeaky clean. One
would think he was a college student by his personal appearance.
These damn kids today are just so complex and sophisticated in
their thinking that it would take an army of psychologists and
scientists to figure them out. They're a product of their
environment, which is a by-product of class structure. When I
think of this, sometimes I question whether my job has any real
validation or purpose to it. I'm out there on the streets trying to put
a stop to the madness we see every day. But what about the
controlling figures in our society who the people elect and put in
power? These are the real crooks and madmen. Sometimes I just
want to say fuck it, let it all go to hell. But then, for my children I
realize that either you're part of the problem, or part of the
solution." Stopping abruptly, he wondered what the hell he was
saying. It seemed like he was just rambling on as if talking in his
sleep.

For a minute, she did not know what to say. His conversation
totally caught her off guard because he had never revealed this side
of himself to her before. As a matter of fact, he would make a good
social worker, probation officer or politician, she thought. The
thought made her laugh.

Offended he asked, "What's so funny?"

Still laughing, she replied with tears streaming down her face, "I was just thinking that you were in the wrong profession. Maybe you should run for some type of office, or become a social worker. Something where you'd feel that you were making a difference." Straightening herself up, she continued, "I always wondered how you really felt about your job. And I never knew that you were so social and politically conscious. Well, I'm surprised to say the least."

The scowl on his face changed to a more relaxed look as he thought about her reply.

"Well, there's a lot about me that you don't know, Ms. Simmons. I'm a detective not a psychologist, so there are plenty of things that I do not even know about myself."

Thinking about this, she stated, "It seems like that with most of us, detective." Pausing again, she went on. "I was just calling to give you a little insight. And if I think about anything else I'll give you a call, okay?" She wanted to continue their conversation, but just did not know what else to say. He was feeling the same way. Yet, at the same time he did not want to open up a can of worms. After all, he was a married man. So why seek to rekindle what they could not keep burning?

After hanging up the phone, the detective tossed the covers aside and jumped out of bed. Another day as a police officer was about to start.

Chapter Ten

Grabbing his pager and seeing that seven, sevens came across the screen put him on point, letting him know that he was going to receive a phone call on his cellular phone within the next minute or so.

Two minutes later, his phone went off. "Who's this?" he asked.

"Yo, meet me at the end of the path, on the side by your house. I'll be there at ten-thirty."

Before Steve could reply, the person on the other end hung up on him.

For the first time since Boom's killing, a sense of uneasiness came over him. His heart began to beat fast, and his mind wandered in and out of thought. For a minute, he became delirious and didn't know whether to trust the cat on the other line, but he needed the rest of his loot.

To be on the safe side, Steve decided to himself to come armed and prepared for the worst although deep inside he hoped that nothing went wrong. But things had already gone wrong, and he could ignore that fact a one minute. He witnessed with his own eyes his cousin getting cut down like a soldier in one of those army flicks.

The cat on the other end had already planned out what he wanted to do. Now it was just the point of gathering up the coverage to complete the task. It had been an hour since he smoked the last blunt. The marijuana had him in an uncaring state of mind. The more he thought about what he was going to do, the more hyped up he became to get it done. Time seemed to be an illusion;

the only thing that seemed real at the moment was the feel of the nine-millimeter baby Glock in the right pocket of his flight jacket.

When ten o'clock rolled around, both figures seemed to be caught up in the same movements, as if reading the other's thoughts. Steve placed a 44 Magnum Desert Eagle in his waistline, while the other cat took his nine out his jacket, placing it in his waistline. Both were in deep concentration and stone-faced, wondering just how the situation was going to play out.

Walking out of the house, the man leaving to meet Steve got in the rental, pulling out the driveway before shifting into drive and speeding off, causing the tires to chirp as they skipped across the pavement. Steve, on the other hand, stepped out of his front door and sat on the porch contemplating his next move.

At about ten-fifteen, Steve began walking out of his front gate, bopping down the block. He lived in a middle-class neighborhood, so by this time every night not a soul could be seen on the streets, except occasionally, when someone would go to the neighborhood 7-11 around the block, or if someone was on their way back home. Other than that, it was so quiet you could hear the faintest sign of noise. That was exactly how it was at the moment. Steve could hear his breathing and his pants rubbing as his legs moved back and fourth causing the fabric on both sides of his thighs.

It was a little chilly out, and he was glad that at the last moment, he decided to put on a light jacket because he sure as hell would have wished he had. It wasn't winter yet, but because of the dampness when he exhaled, his breath formed smoke rings as it hit the air. At the edge of the road and at the mouth of the path, houses stood on both sides. He was in a dark, wooded area, so it was hard for him to see ahead, but during the day one could see that the path clearing was wide enough to fit a car through if one decided to drive through the length of it.

Steve shivered a little as he stood in the darkness with both hands inside the front of his pants. His right hand grasped the handle of the large gun, which practically extended all the way down the side of his leg. The surface of it felt cold as it pressed against his skin. Bringing his left hand up to look at his watch, he could see that it was now ten-thirty. A chill crept through him as he sought to compose himself.

The other figure was already halfway through the path with a small flashlight, searching his way through the brush and looking for level ground to walk on. The marijuana had him keen and on point. It seemed like his eyesight and hearing improved as he focused and listened to everything in the surrounding woods around him. It was weird, he thought to himself, he couldn't remember the last time he heard birds chirping and flying about through the trees during the late night. As he stepped from the street into the brush, he noticed the temperature dropped dramatically the further he reached into the woods. Adrenaline pumped through his veins like hot water, and his mind was in such a frenzy that the cold did not bother him in the least as he walked on. He wore all black from head to toe, down to the gloves on his hands. A black baseball cap covered his head as the hood from his sweatshirt enveloped the baseball cap, revealing only a shadow of his face.

Something in the distance caught Steve's attention as he watched the surrounding woods for anyone approaching. A small beam of light could be seen swaying in the distance, as if someone was using a flashlight to find his or her way. As he looked closely, he could see that there was a figure in the distance as the flashlight cut off and the person stepped out into the wide path, which was lit up by the moon. Not wanting to reveal himself yet, he decided to just stand in the cut and await the oncoming figure.

The other figure had caught a glimpse of him as well, and from his memory in the he pretty much knew Steve's body structure, so he was sure it was him and stepped up the pace.

He said nothing as he came within three yards of Steve, but instead took full observation of the scenery around them before throwing the envelope filled with hundreds on the ground. The swelled envelope hit the front of Steve's right boot before toppling to the dust.

In the same moment Steve bent over to pick up the envelope, he heard the clicking sound of an automatic being cocked back as if loading a bullet into the chamber. This was a sound he knew all too well from his own dealings with the machinery. Before he could look up and take his eyes away from the envelope, the figure told him, "Get on your knees, place your hands behind your head, and interlock your fingers together." And with extra emphasis and conviction, he stated, "And don't say a fucking word!"

Immediately, Steve started to tremble, dropping to his knees and placing both hands to his head. He thought about running, but then decided against this idea, figuring that it would definitely get him killed. He wanted to talk, but instead, he listened and felt his pee soaking his pants and running onto the ground forming a puddle. This did not bother him though, all he wanted to do was save his life. Maybe he could talk his way out of this, he decided.

"Why are you doing this? I did my part; I gave you what you wanted. What else do you want? Y'all can't kill every motherfucker in the world!"

Before he could go on with any more rhetoric, the figure in black pointed the nine directly at him. He thought about shooting Steve when he first started speaking, but he found his squirming amusing. Plus, he wanted to let the worm know exactly why this was happening to him.

Smiling at Steve, and showing a mouth full of gold-capped teeth, he started to speak in a low tone, still pointing the gun toward him.

"You know why I'm doing this you little bitch. If you'd cross your own blood, then you'll cross anyone else. You think we'd trust you to go about your business and keep things quiet?" Shaking his head from side to side, the figure again went on. "You don't think we're that stupid. The money means nothing. That shit gets made every minute of the day. As long as there are crack heads, there's crack money." Pointing at the envelope he went on, "As a matter of fact, I'm gonna kill you and leave the money right there where it's laying right now."

Laughing once again, he paused before continuing, "Bitch ass niggers like you fuck the game up. You're such a bitch! You mother fuckers make it hard for cats like me to do our thing." As he started to laugh, once again, the fear that Steve felt started to be replaced by anger. In so many words, he had been told that he was going to be murdered regardless. So it really didn't matter because the end result was going to be the same anyway. I might as well go out with a bang, he thought to himself as he watched the man in front of him laugh continuously in a mocking manner.

Taking his hand from the back of his head, he tried to reach for the 44 magnum in his waistline as he screamed, "Fuck you!"

"No fuck you, snake!" was all that was heard before the echo of three gunshots rumbled like thunder throughout the air. One man lay in the street, while the figure standing placed his signature of death inside the pouch of his sweatshirt and began to run. Within seconds of the incident, sounds of sirens filled the area. But it was too late because he had made it through the path to his car. Taking a minute to catch his breath, he mumbled, "God, what am I becoming?" before jumping into his Park Avenue and pulling back onto the parkway.

His adrenaline and heart were pumping so fast that for a minute, he thought he could actually hear his blood flow. His heart was beating so hard against his chest that he began to feel a little pain. Both hands on the steering wheel shook as he tried his best keep a tight grip. With his right foot pressed heavily on the foot pedal, he accelerated the car to 90mph, 45mph over the speed limit. Passing underneath a two-lane bridge he noticed there was a state trooper backed up along the grass just beyond the bridge as he passed through.

For a minute, as the car drove past the state trooper, the trooper paid no attention. But then after realizing how fast the vehicle was moving as 94mph clocked on his radar gun, he decided to pursue. Flicking on the lights and sirens he stepped on the pedal causing the car to slide a little as it came off the grass onto the paved parkway. The .350 horsepower engine went to work automatically and within seconds, the trooper was within eyesight of the vehicle. Tailing it from 3 yards back, he concentrated on the digits on the license plate so that he could call it into headquarters just in case he needed back up. Once this was accomplished, he stepped up the pace to align his car right in back of the vehicle. This seemed to serve no purpose because the driver did not seem to be responding; instead he began picking up more speed.

The driver knew it was essential to get away. Plus, he was not sure whether the trooper was on him because of the situation which took place ten minutes earlier or because he was caught speeding. One thing was for sure, he was not taking any chances. At the moment, all he could think about was getting away and nothing else mattered. It was all about survival of the fittest.

Looking through the rearview mirror as he drove, he could see the state trooper's car a few feet away from the rear bumper. "Pull over to the side of the road" the trooper ordered as he sought to pass the car from the back toward the driver side. By this time, the assailant already held his nine in his right hand and began firing at the state trooper's car over his left shoulder without bothering to roll down the window. Five shots erupted at a rapid pace, sounding like quarter sticks of dynamite. Two of the rounds hit their mark; one hit the trooper in the shoulder and the other bullet hit him in the left side of his neck, automatically causing him to lose control of the police vehicle. The car went sprawling out of control onto the surrounding lawn, continuing to build up speed down into the woods before crashing head on into a tree. The impact smashed the front like a slice of white bread folding in half. A boom was followed by smoke, and then flames followed.

As he drove, he did not see or witness the outcome of the trooper's car. Yet, he could imagine it and was thankful that it was not him to say the least. Well, it really didn't matter because at this point, he realized the situation was not good for him at all. There was no time to be scared or think too long, now it was pure instinct kicking in. For a minute, he actually toyed with the idea of blowing his own head off, but then quickly discarded this from his mind because, as a Five Percenter, he was taught that suicide was the act of a coward and the ultimate sin that any man can make against the Creator; real men accept their fates. By this time in the game, he was now sure that death in the worst way was his fate, especially once he killed that state trooper a quarter mile back. For sure, they had road blocks set up ahead at the next exit. He really thought about turning back around, but through the rearview mirror he could see flashing lights in the distance, acknowledging this, he realized that turning back was not an option.

A quarter of a mile away, a heavily armed squad of about twenty police officers stood wearing black task force uniforms with bullet proof vests over their under their jackets. They stood around squad cars positioned in a barricade. Some were armed with semi-automatic Glocks, while the snipers positioned behind the first row of cars all carried 12-gauge shotguns. It was their duty to stop the assailant by picking him off before he reached the barricade. It was already foretold that one police officer was down, and that the assailant was armed and extremely dangerous. So safety, caution, and the utilization of extreme force, was the necessary measure. These were the orders that were given by the commander at the headquarters of the 4th precinct to the sergeant on scene. In plain terms, what he was saying was that at all costs, avoid any more police officers lives, and if necessary take the assailant out.

The sergeant in charge was a real American patriot, down to the American flag posted on the front of his lawn. If there was one thing he hated as a police officer, more than anything else was an officer dying in the line of duty. He did not need any orders from headquarters to realize what he was going to do, or what policy to take on the matter. It was all in the cards he figured. When a police officer dies, then if possible, the suspect dies also.

Sergeant Lamar personally kept in radio contact with the officers who were in about a twenty-yard distance from the suspect. They were given direct orders by him to keep their distance. No one was to approach the vehicle unless the driver sought to turn around and retreat back toward the opposite direction. Their job was just to monitor his actions and lure him into the roadblock set up by their fellow officers.

Coming within eyesight of the floodlights in the distance ahead all Divine could think about was what the difference would be between spending the rest of his life in jail and being dead. To tell the truth, he could see no difference because being in jail was like being dead. Since he'd come this far, he decided to go all out because there was no other way around it. His life was over, either way. In a mere matter of seconds, he thought about all of his loved ones as time slipped by, the seconds seemed like hours.

Driving as slow as he could, he took one more look at the patrol cars through the rearview mirror. Right then, he decided to flee on foot. Keeping the gear in drive, he opened the passenger door and rolled onto the pavement, continuing onto the grass. With giant strides, he ran toward the surrounding woods as the police jumped out of their squad cars with Glocks outstretched, chasing this shadow down. Within minutes, Sergeant Lamar and his squad were also on the scene, along with a helicopter, which hovered above, providing them with light so they could follow the suspects every move.

Once Divine was in the woods, he struggled through the tall grass and wild brush. There was nowhere to hide with the large floodlight shining down from the helicopter. For a minute, it felt like he was going crazy. Frantically, he ran in circles, busting shots up at the helicopter until there were no more bullets in the clip. He was caught up in the frenzy to the point where he did not realize the dark blue unformed men who surrounded him. Then he heard, "Throw the gun down, and turn around slowly. You're under arrest!" At that moment, his recollection of life passed right before his eyes; he knew he had to play this part out to the end He figured he was a dead man regardless of what happened tonight. Life in prison did not appeal to him at all.

Tears began to stream out of the assailant's eyes. And as he turned around and got cut down by the slugs of 30 or so officers' Glocks, he remembered hearing the screams "Put the gun down! We have you surrounded! Put the gun---" The sound of gun fire going off like firecrackers could be heard a quarter mile away as they harpooned through his body, causing his feet to lift off the ground sending his mangled frame sprawling into the air.

For the next few seconds, everything fell silent as the floodlight from the helicopter made the remains of the assailant's body easily visible to the naked eye from several yards away. All of the officers looked at one another before laying eyes on Sergeant Lamar as he looked on with approval and satisfaction. A broad smile covered his face; it was as if he sincerely enjoyed the night's killing.

"Let's clear out!" he ordered as the crime scene unit moved in to seal off the area.

Divine was as dead as a doorknob, blood and earth covered his remains like artificial turf.

*   *   *   *   *

The next morning Blaze, Detective Aldoe, and Detective Jackson, as well as Frank and his partner Speedy, were glued to the TV watching the eight o'clock news. The detectives were in the confines of the senior detectives office. And Officer Frank and his partner Speedy sat at the neighborhood diner drinking coffee and eating donuts as they watched Steve's blanketed body come up on the screen being carried away by paramedics. And then, Divine's Polaroid picture was shown on the screen stating that he was a possible suspect in the case. They also showed about three minutes of footage of him being pursued by state troopers and police before being gunned down.

Blaze was dumbfounded by what he saw on the TV screen and all he felt like doing was lying down. He needed time to think about future moves that had to be made.

He was too dazed to even bother to shut the TV off as he laid back on the sofa wondering to himself. Placing both hands over his face, he closed his eyes and dipped into deep thought.

The sergeant and detective, on the other hand, both sat and wondered about the connection between Steve, who they knew was Boom's cousin, and Divine, who they did not realize was a member of MPR. Pondering, neither of them said a word.

Looking at the television, Detective Aldoe said, "This shit is getting interesting…how all these bodies are turning up. It seems that anyone who had anything to do with that investigation concerning the Brotherhood has gotten popped. But I'd like to know what part Steve played in all this? Supposedly, from the witnesses accounts, he fits the description of the person who was kidnapped during Boom's murder at that McDonald's parking a lot." Pausing for a moment to take a sip of coffee from his #1 Dad mug, he continued, "But why didn't they kill him in the parking lot with his cousin? Why wait a day later?"

Scratching his head as he looked at his younger partner intently, he fell silent, scratching his head in bewilderment as his partner looked on in utter confusion.

*   *   *   *   *

Inside a neighborhood diner called Expresso Café, Officer Frank and his partner Speedy sat on high stools stationed around the counter as many people surrounded the atmosphere. Some sitting at the counter on the stools just like them, while others sat at tables. Everyone was glued to the TV this morning, as information about the three killings filled the screen. The third killing was that of the state trooper. Amongst themselves, Frank and his partner began to speak about the matter freely, as if no on else was around. They both knew Divine was a hustler, but neither of them could picture him killing anyone. The pretty boy persona just did not match up.

Frank was kind of upset by what he saw and heard on the television. From what he knew of Divine, he didn't think he was a bad kid at all. He was just a kid caught up in bad circumstances. Speedy, on the other hand, expressed no sympathy for the man or what happened. He felt he got his just do. Plus, he was accused of killing an officer, so as far as Speedy was concerned, there was nothing more to think about. At one point in their conversation, he questioned Frank's sincerity for the law. There was no use in arguing the point because they both knew their ideologies were like day and night.

Walking out of the diner as if the conversation never took place, both officers laughed and joked with one another about how ignorant they thought the other was to the realities of the world.

Chapter Eleven

It was beautiful on the day of Divine's burial, and the type of weather that anyone could enjoy. Birds and bees flew about. Even squirrels could be seen frolicking and acting playful as they jumped here and about from tree limbs, like little kids having fun on a school playground.

The cemetery was crowded to the point it seemed like whole neighborhood was gathered in one small place. People came from the Bronx and as far as eastern Long Island, as well as many other states like Virginia, Georgia, and Connecticut, to pay their respect to the slain hood superstar.

Benze's, Lexus' and all types of other fancy sedans lined the streets. Every major hustler in the tri-state area was present, and so were teams of plain-clothed police and undercover federal agents.

During a law enforcement engagement after the state trooper's funeral, which was held the day before Divine's, a special task force was set up to look into the matter more closely. Even the mayor and governor expressed concern, vowing to the state trooper's wife and family that there would be an investigation and justice. This special unit was to be governed by the police commissioner himself at One Police Plaza in Manhattan. Once again, Sergeant Cormier was to head this unit in the field.

There were so many individuals present at Divine's funeral, that it would have been virtually impossible to point out the undercovers who watched, observed, and listened intently to every detail and conversation, which took place.

Just beyond the trees in the distance, Sergeant Cormier, along with Officer Gomez, took pictures of all the occupants at the funeral. They each must have snapped about twenty-six shots apiece, making sure not to miss anyone in the enormous group. This was done with precision and in a matter of five minutes. Then they rushed off to ensure that they were not eyed by anyone.

Blaze was on point the whole morning and couldn't help but to feel that someone was watching him. To his surprise, as he searched the surrounding area to put his intuition at ease, he noticed movement from the corner of his eye in the far distance. Turning around to look toward the movement, he saw two figures wearing all black and sporting field jackets, walking off in the distance. "That's the beast," he thought silently. He wondered what they were doing here at the cemetery. Just as these thoughts seeped into his mind, two figures approached him. Standing on either side of him stood Freedom and Jasheem, "Peace! They stated as Freedom looked on past Blaze, locking eyes on a figure.

Blaze could see by the look in their eyes that they both were kind of edgy. They were standing there tense, as if something was truly troubling them. He understood the mood though, because he felt exactly the same. The last year and a half had been a full of ups and downs for everyone affiliated with the family. Especially for him, since his life had changed overnight from living at his mother's house to the streets, and then becoming a part of something bigger than he could have ever imagined. At the present moment, the Brotherhood was in danger of becoming extinct. Question marks existed in all three of their minds, and for good reason too.

Twenty minutes later, the ceremony was over and Divine's casket was being lowered into the six-foot hole in the ground. As this took place, everyone began to disperse in groups to their vehicles. Almost everyone present knew Freedom, Jasheem, and Blaze so crowds swarmed around the three as pounds, handshakes, and hugs poured out to them from every direction. Lots of people passed out phone numbers to the trio to keep in contact, some for business, while others were just to extend courtesy.

Everyone who was directly affiliated with MPR and the Brotherhood gathered around one another. Even though talk was exchanged back and fourth, no words were said to express the loss that everyone felt. There had to be about thirty young brothers in all.

Pulling Blaze to the side, Jasheem and Freedom introduced him to Papo. At first look, one would think he was black, but after hearing him speak it became apparent right away that he was Hispanic. When he first greeted Blaze, even he was taken back by the accent because he looked just like another brother to him. He would have never suspected him to be a Spanish cat. Not that it mattered, but from all the dealings in the business, all he ever came across were brothers because the Brotherhood kept their business, for the most part, an all black operation.

Shaking hands, the young Latin spoke first. Every word uttered had a little accent to it although his pronunciation was very good, which meant he'd had formal schooling of some kind. Smiling to Blaze he uttered, "So you're Blaze, I heard a lot of good things about you from our two friends here and I hope that we can do business together cuz I think it can be a beautiful thing for the both of us. They have my number so when you need to get in contact with me, feel free to use it, okay?" With that, the young Latin broke off from the group nodding his head at Jasheem and Freedom before disappearing as quickly as he showed up.

The trio watched the man as he walked off into the crowd disappearing. Turning their attention back to one another, Blaze was the first one to say something "I know that guy has to be a millionaire, word is bond!"

To this statement both Jasheem and Freedom smirked, nodding their heads up and down in unison before Freedom stated, "Yeah, without question, gee. That little young ass Dominican got cream, for real! The motherfucker's got direct access to the shit from their country; the shit comes from Columbia right to the islands. We pay twenty thousand a kilo, when he probably pays eight thousand at the most. And that's after getting the shit here to New York. I'd be a millionaire too, if I had a connect like that. That's why the game is fucked up for blacks because we have to go through everyone else to get our hands on it. We are the last ones on the totem pole, and we're the ones paying the hardest price because the so called war against drugs is being fought in our communities when whites represent 90% of drug use in America."

As Freedom finished talking, all three dwelt on what was just said before Jasheem started talking, "God, these devils know what they're doing. Right now we're in the age of crack, but this shit started a long time ago, way back in the Vietnam War days when they were bringing opium and heroin back in the country in dead soldier bodies. At the time, you had the Black Consciousness Movement going on with the Nation of Islam, the Black Liberation Army, The Black Panthers, and the N.A.A.C.P. These mother fuckers seen that black people were starting to wake up and get themselves together. Now, you know they couldn't have that, so the government, along with the mafia, yeah, them pizza-eating peckerwoods started bringing heroin into black neighborhoods. And before you knew it, heroin addiction was an epidemic in the ghettos. Of course, the devils didn't mind as long as the shit stayed in our neighborhoods, fucking us up. But now, it is thirty years later, and the drug is crack. The only difference is that now their people are messed up on the shit just like ours. I guess they didn't realize that crack does not discriminate one bit."

Laughing, he went on, "It's the drug of choice for the rich and poor. Fuck them, let some of them mother fuckers die to. In Washington, DC, like two blocks from the White House there's crack spots everywhere. Mad white motherfuckers be pulling up in Benzes and all types of shit to buy product. At first, I couldn't believe it when I went down there. I was like nah, them mother fuckers are police! But then when I seen cats keep serving them, I was like, oh shit! Even them fucking whities in the white house smoke crack. Word, shit is crazy. Now they waging war against us like we bring the shit in this country when we're the last ones to touch the shit. We have to get our money and get outta this shit soon because it's nothing but a set up. They can stop Haitians from coming into this country, but they can't stop cargo planes and freighters filled with coke from getting here. Yeah right, these devils are capitalists to their heart; this country was built on crime. All they think about is money, if it's about a dollar then it makes sense to them. That's how it is, they don't give a fuck who pays the price, and they'll sacrifice one of their own to kill two of us." After stating all this, he began to chuckle, shaking his head. He continued to laugh, but Blaze could see the irony in this.

No one said anything else for the next few moments; with fixed eyes they all watched the quiet scenery of the surrounding cemetery. Everything was peaceful, except for the pile of parked cars behind one another seeking to depart. Within five minutes, everything cleared and the only people around were the three of them and the grounds people attending to Divine's plot.

As the three walked off, they all looked back at Divine's place of burial, and for a second, Blaze caught the chills as sensations crept up his spine. Getting buried to him seemed like the most violent part about death. He didn't want to think about anyone throwing dirt on top of him, sealing his fate for eternity.

Walking to Freedom's royal blue New Yorker, Blaze stated, "Damn, we came a long way!" These words caused both Freedom and Jasheem to stop in their tracks to look at their companion as he spoke. "I remember three years ago when I never had more than one hundred dollars in my pocket at one time. I used to look up to Supreme because ever since we were young, he had everything cuz his cousins were in the game. And then when he was like fifteen, he was already doing his thing. He was the only black kid in junior high with a new car. And then when he started showing me shit, he put me down with everything as if I was his little brother." As he stopped speaking he looked into the sky, tilting his head so that the suns rays beat on his face and neck. "Word, him and Infinite were my niggers, them cats taught me everything that I know about the game. And then the shit with Takim, Kariem and the rest of the family…"

Before Blaze could say anything else, Freedom placed his right hand on Blaze's shoulder, stating, "God, that's the way shit is, life's like that. Life and death is all around us at all times, there's no way out of this shit until we perish. But I'll be damned if I'm a be broke, that's for sure. These devils are not the only ones who have to eat, shit; I like the life of luxury too. That's the bottomline, gee, either you're gonna have, or be one of the have nots. Every day is a battle, and we're all in this one way or another, whether we like it or not." He dug his hands in his right pants pocket, pressing the little button on the key chain to turn off the cars alarm before placing the key in the door. After the door was unlocked, Jasheem got in on the passenger side, while Blaze got in the back behind Freedom.

No one spoke as Freedom took the New Yorker 55 miles an hour, cruising the streets, but never exceeding the town speed limit. Everyone's mind was deep in thought, dwelling upon the past and present recorded history. Each of them wondered what the other was thinking; yet none of them asked or even looked at the other. Their faces were of stone, expressionless despite their concern and question about the future.

*　　*　　*　　*　　*

The sound of typewriters clicking and clacking could be heard over everything else in the busy office area. Usually, there would be groups of people huddled around one another chatting and gossiping. But today, the tension that existed was overwhelming because of the meeting, which was about to take place.

Sergeant Cormier sat behind a desk with both legs propped up. A pile of notes and pictures sat directly in front of him, as he sifted through the compiled information slowly taking mental notes of everything he set his eyes upon. He smiled as he thought about what he'd uncovered; he'd found exactly what he was looking for.

The sound of someone banging on the door awoke him out of his thoughts as he looked up to see the door wide open and Officer Thomas, one of his assistants on the case, standing in front of him wide-mouthed and donning a grin from ear to ear. "They're ready for you," he blurted out. His superior smiled back, and damn near tripped as he hurried to remove his outstretched legs from the desk while trying to gather up all the case paraphernalia into a portfolio. Standing up, he said nothing; instead, he chose to take inventory of his clothing, fixing his tie before choosing to follow the officer out into the adjoining corridor.

The sound of two individual foot patterns clanking on the tiled floor filled the hallway like music echoing against the surrounding walls. Once the officer opened the door, all noise became oblivious to Sergeant. Cromier as he entered the room, acknowledging the familiar faces and sudden stares that welcomed him. About ten individuals in all, including the police commissioner, awaited him. The commissioner sat at the far right end of the three adjoined rectangular tables. Some of the other individuals were police officers and secretaries, while others wore suits, which signified they were men of importance. Notebook pads and pens were positioned out in front of everyone.

The sergeant neither said anything, nor looked at any of the individuals sitting as he strolled into the room making a right, and walking straight to the black board. Looking above his head, he pulled down a screen, which extended four feet down, reaching just below the black board. After pulling the overhead projector out of the corner and placing it directly in front of the middle of the screen, he plugged the chord into the socket, causing the screen to light up bright white. He then turned around with the portfolio held tightly in his hand. Striving to seem as if he was in deep thought, he ran his fingers through his hair with his left hand, looked at everyone briefly, and then began. "Good afternoon gentlemen, for those of you who do not know me, my name is Sergeant. Cromier." Smiling, he added, "Now, if we can skip all the formalities, I'd like to get down to business. My team and me have been keeping the subjects under surveillance, and in fact, seem to know the identity and whereabouts of all the key members of the Brotherhood. We were able to obtain this information through pictures that were taken by me and Officer Gomez at the funeral of Doug Harrison, also known as Divine, who was an affiliate and high ranking member of the group up until the time of his death."

Walking over to the desk where an empty seat sat next to the commissioner's, he poured contents from the portfolio onto the top of the desk. Grabbing one picture in particular, he paced back to the overhead projector placing the picture down on the clear plastic surface causing it to reflect onto the screen. Turning straight toward the group, he stated, "Ladies and gents, these seem to be the three remaining heads of the organization known as the Brotherhood." Pointing a finger at each one, he went on, "This is Jermaine Jackson, AKA Blaze, this guy here is Tyrone Willis AKA Freedom, and this here is Osiris Arnold, known to everyone as Jasheem." Pointing toward Jasheem's reflection he added, "This guy right here is going to be our key to breaking the whole operation. The word on the streets is that he is the major supplier of weight to the neighborhood dealers, in approximately ten towns in Long Island, various parts of Queens, and the Bronx. He even does a lot of business in other north eastern states; instead of taking a trip to Manhattan, he gives it to them at three to four dollars more a gram, and saves them the possibility of being robbed by stick up kids, or caught by police. As it turns out, we have someone who is in custody right now in the Nassau County jail who is a friend of the subjects, and who I'm sure will be willing to purchase narcotics from Jasheem for us in exchange for his current charges being thrown out. At the moment, he is incarcerated for selling 500 grams of crack cocaine to one of our undercovers and faces a six to life sentence since this is his second felony drug offense. Therefore, I'm more than sure that some deal can be worked out in exchange for him doing us this little favor." Chuckling and crossing his fingers in front of him, he asked to no one in particular, "Are there any questions?" The room began to get loud as everyone began to talk to one another in half whispers; it only seemed loud because of all the voices speaking at once.

Looking at the pile of pictures on the desk, the commissioner asked, "Sergeant, when can we expect to see this case come to a close?" As he finished his question, his eyes seemed to pierce right through the sergeant's air of coolness, leaving him feeling a little edgy. For a minute, he almost stuttered as he sought to answer the commissioner's question.

But almost as quickly as he lost his cool, he regained it, once again replying, "Commissioner, I feel that within two months, at the most, we should have the situation rapped up. And—"

Before he could continue, the commissioner cut him off. "I do not care how you do it, but the mayor and governor are all over my back because it's election time. So, the bottom line is, I need results as soon as possible." Getting up from the table he walked toward the door as his two assistants and an officer followed. "And I need results before two months!" he blurted out, just before stepping through the doorway. The sergeant looked around the room into the remaining faces. He grabbed his chin, rubbing the two day unshaved skin. "Excuse me everyone," the sergeant stated, following the assistant out into the hallway.

Perspiration filled the lining of the sergeant's shirt under the armpits, causing him to feel a little uncomfortable. Pulling on the front of his shirt, he sought to stop the material from sticking to his skin. Exhaling heavily, both of his hands clumsily sought to release the tension from the tie around his neck. After removing the tie, he unfastened the first two buttons on the loosely fitting flannel shirt.

The hallway seemed to him to be even longer now that he was leaving than when he first entered earlier that morning. As he looked straight ahead, at the back of his assistant's head, he wondered how many minutes had passed by.

"Finally," he sighed as they reached the front doors. As he stood on the pavement, he looked up into the sky delighting in the beauty of the day. For a minute, he began to daydream, but was awakened hastily by a car pulling next to the curb. It was his assistant. "Another dreary day of work," he thought as he got in on the passenger side of the car, slamming the door. At once, his assistant punched the car into drive, pulling away from the curb into awaiting traffic.

*   *   *   *   *

Cigar smoke filled the small office. Detective Aldoe puffed away at his Havana cigar, enjoying the richness of its taste in his mouth. He only enjoyed a Havana every once in a while, occasionally treating himself to the expensive Cuban product, on any ordinary day, a regular cigar would do. Rings of smoke lingered throughout the room in clouds, visibly dimming the bright-lit area. This did not bother him at all; as a matter of fact, he loved the recreation of smoking the sweet smelling cigar and wished he could do it often.

Two knocks came at the shabby hollow door then Detective Jackson walked in with a half-hearted smirk on his face, revealing even, bright white teeth in contrast to his dark complexion. As he entered the room, the cigar stench hit him squarely in his face, almost causing the man to choke before he placed two fingers to his nose, pinching both nostrils. The young detective did not smoke, so he was not fond of the smell at all, and made no reservations about revealing it. Catching his breath, he stated to the senior officer, "The captain wants to see us in his office, pronto."

The older officer shook his head, smashing the ashy burning tip of the cigar into the ashtray. "I wonder what the jerk wants now." he sneered as he looked at the black detective. "I wonder what the fuck we did wrong now." he said, more as a general statement than as a question, but Detective Jackson didn't stick around to answer anyway. He was already out of the room and away from the cigar's stench, which he did not want on his clothing.

Entering the spacious opulent room, Detective Aldoe could not help but to notice the sweet aroma of pipe tobacco, and for a minute, he delighted in the smell as it teased his nostrils. After closing the door, he and the younger detective stood at the foot of the captain's large desk. Captain Rozak, a placard sitting on the front of the desk read. This the sergeant couldn't help but to notice even before he took one look at the small, frail figure leaning back in the large leather chair. The two men were not on good terms at all, and the sergeant heated the respect that he had to show this man who was his superior by rank. He felt that the captain was both arrogant and disrespectful.

Captain Rozak, from the moment both detectives entered his office, studied them with a fixed demonic stare, smiling as if he knew something that they didn't. He loved the power and control he wielded over everyone in the precinct, especially Sergeant Aldoe, who he felt was nothing but an overrated detective, who should be doing nothing more than beating his feet on the street.

Within minutes, all three figures were locked in a staring stance until the captain spoke up. He possessed a weird smirk on his face as he began to speak as if he were making an important speech, "Well, I'd hate to bust your bubble fellas but that little investigation that y'all had concerning the so called Brotherhood gang or whatever you call them, from this day on is discontinued! And-"

Just as he was about to continue, Sergeant Aldoe tried to interject something, but all he managed to get out was "But, captain." before the captain cut him down.

The captain continued, saying, "But nothing, the orders came from the commissioner himself this morning. A special task force has been set up to investigate. And our orders are to stay out of their way!" Staring at the sergeant head on, he added "And there will be serious reprimands for anyone who does not follow these orders! Now, go find some other thugs to bring to justice!" His last words caused him to chuckle a bit as he picked up his pipe from its holder, struck a match, and set fire to the wooden object.

There was no use saying anything else to the man, so the senior detective stormed out the door, slamming it behind him before Detective Jackson could even step in behind him. The younger detective looked at the captain before shaking his head, exhaling, and exiting to leave the smirking captain to enjoy the stench of his pipe.

Chapter Twelve

The surrounding neighborhood corners were empty of the crowds of young people who were usually be present on such a nice weekend afternoon. Even though it was fall, the weather felt like summer was still trying to stick around a little while longer.

The blocks were empty because everyone was at the town park. Back to back basketball games ensued, while kids played tag, running around the park as their mothers watched, enjoying in the fun and laughter, and gossiping amongst themselves.

Cars were parked along the curb on the strip outside the park. Most of the cars were empty of occupants but some were occupied. Music blasted out of the trunks of some, leaving a sound of mixed melodies as all the different sounds hit the air. In the middle of the street a ce-lo game took place. This was a regular activity at the park every day for all the big willy hustlers from the neighborhood. Gambling was a form of relaxation for the group. Aside from making money and dealing with politics of the streets, this served as a way to release some steam and have fun at the same time. It depended on who played, but on some days, up to ten thousand dollars existed in the game's bank. While on most days, any bet could be placed, usually they started with ten dollars.

The park was crowded to say the least, and many things went on, some illegal and some things were just part of the park's activities. Two figures stood discussing their business, paying no attention to what was going on around them.

"Yo, sun, it's like this. One key costs twenty thousand. Now if you buy two or more, he'll give them to you for seventeen a piece. Wc make thirty-three thousand off one key selling it in the way that I explained on paper, selling every gram and a half for fifty dollars. What you do is supply the shorties on the block and they'll make one hundred off what you give them for fifty. Let them deal with the fiends and the hot ass corners, all you do is supply them. Off a key you'll make thirteen thousand profit, and that's enough to buy a key and a half, and plus still have money to spend." Smiling at the figure next to him before taking a guzzle of the one liter spring water in his right hand, he stated, "I guarantee you in a couple of months, you'll have no less than three and a half kilos."

Contemplating this as he smiled, Blaze looked around the park, taking in Jasheem's words like they were music to his ears.

"Yeah, god, I'm a put the guns down for a little while and see what the deal is with this hustling shit. I'm a drop a call to Papo later on, so we can probably vibe tomorrow on that, word. I have to do something because Rachel can't take this shit no more. We just started talking again, so I'm a slow it down a bit, hustle this shit and maybe go to school.

Jasheem didn't reply he just looked Blaze over, smiling before turning toward his car to make sure all was good, and that no foul play was taking place with his car's system. This park was known as an area where people's cars got jacked for their systems. "Shit!" he exclaimed, remembering he had to meet someone. Looking confused, he stated, "Blaze, I forgot I have to get up with this cat at two to handle some business, so I'm a check you, ah-right."

The two brothers shook hands and gave one another a hug. "Tap me on my pager tomorrow, god." Jasheem stated as the two walked off to their cars.

*   *   *   *   *

Sitting on his stoop, he dialed the number of the person he was seeking. His stomach was tied up in knots and he was nervous, but he had to go through with the plan. He took in a deep breath as the line on the other end rang. On the third ring, the other party picked up, "What's the deal?"

"It's me, god, I'm at the crib so swing by."

"I'll be there in twenty minutes, gee" was all that was said before a dial tone could be heard.

He felt bad about the whole situation, yet he was in deep shit and needed to save his own ass. He had a lot to lose, two children, a wife, home, bank account, and numerous material assets, including two cars, a truck, and a motorcycle. He was not about to sacrifice any of this for anyone. Contemplating the pros and cons of the situation automatically put him at ease. It's either him or me, was how it came down in his mind. Self-preservation was the name of the game now.

True to his word, within seventeen minutes of their conversation on the phone, Jasheem pulled up in a new Jimmy Blazer. Born gazed at the truck with admiration as he walked over to the passenger side and jumped in. Exchanging pounds, they hugged one another playfully, just as they did when they were childhood friends.

"Gee, I heard you made bail." Jasheem stated.

"Yeah, they finally dropped it down to twenty thousand." Born replied, shaking his head and striving to look as serious as possible.

"So what you gonna do now, cowboy?" Jasheem asked.

Giving the impression that he was in deep thought, Born replied, "I gotta do my thang just in case I have to do a couple of years. You know I have to make sure my wife and seeds are gonna be straight. That's why I called you. I gotta get my hustle on without hesitation, word is bond! I wanna cop 500 grams. Do you think you can get that to me?"

Smiling, Jasheem stated, "What, you know you're talking to the man. What type of question is that? Man, I'll have it to you in an hour." Pausing momentarily he added, "Right now the price is 24 a gram."

Feeling satisfied Born replied, "Alright, gee, I'll take that off your hands. We'll do like we always do, okay."

Jasheem replied, "No doubt, gee."

After giving Jasheem a pound, Born stated, "I'll check you in about an hour, god." before stepping out the jeep and bopping all the way to the front door of his home. Jasheem looked at his childhood friend as he walked off, and wondered for a brief second where their childhood innocence had gone. The years went like light speed, and now they were grown, hustling, and living the life of villains. Life has a way of cheating he thought, but not on this occasion because he vowed to himself that he was going to help Born out the best way that he could. Backing the truck into reverse he slid out of the driveway onto the paved street.

Once Born was inside the confines of his home, he immediately slid on the couch situated in the living room to the right of the front door. Right now, he was a ball of confusion, and his mind was bottled up with conflicting thoughts. With both hands he covered his face and began to cry. Ten minutes later, his face and shirt drenched in tears, he got up and picked up the phone, dialing seven digits. Sucking his teeth and shaking his head in disbelief he listened to the other line ring four times before someone picked up. "Hello, Sergeant Cromier, who's speaking?" The other end of the line fell silent as Born basically choked on his own spit before answering.

"Yo, its me, Born, the shit is about to go down in a hour. You already know the place." Not saying anything else he hung up to continue contemplating what he was doing. At twenty-four dollars a gram he knew he was gonna pay twelve thousand for five hundred grams. Pulling the TV out of the entertainment center, he placed it down on the floor. Sixteen, thousand dollar stacks sat in two piles. Counting carefully, he grabbed twelve stacks, which held one thousand in each bundle, placing six in each side of his Tommy Hilfiger jacket. Feeling satisfied, he set out do what he needed to do.

Sergeant Cromier, along with a team of three, were positioned within ten minutes of the phone call and at the site of where the deal was about to take place. No mistakes were being made if he could help it. Born did not know that since the early morning of his release from the pen, he had been followed and a surveillance team kept tabs on his every movement. One thing was for sure, they were going to make sure that he did not renege on the proposed deal and take flight. The long arm of the law was in full control. They knew before he called that the deal was going down.

Jasheem was already on his way to the meeting place with a half a key. And since he lived in Central Islip, which was a town over from Brentwood, he was able to make it to the train station in a matter of twenty minutes. Coming down Suffolk Avenue, he took full notice of the scenery around him. Traffic was mild and from what he could see, there seemed to be no blue and whites around. Seeing this made him feel safe and secure. Plus, the police did not know him out there like they did in Nassau County, and especially in his hood, the Hempstead Terrace area.

A mix tape with Nas played on, as the Blazer reached the train station entrance along the Suffolk Avenue strip. The glare that was shining through the windshield caused Jasheem to place his left hand over the top of his eyes to block out the rays of sun as he flicked on the left signal and waited for a space to enter the oncoming traffic into the parking lot. About 100 yards ahead was Brentwood Road, which crossed into Suffolk Avenue, so as the light on that road turned green causing Suffolk's to show red, a break in the oncoming traffic allowed Jasheem to make the turn. Once the truck moved onto the entrance, he gave the pedal a little gas, causing the blazer to jerk forward. He drove around the compound once and then proceeded to a parking space in a lot where there were already a lot of cars parked. Since he had a few minutes to spare, he decided to rest because he was fatigued. Pushing the control on the door console to lower the seat back, he looked around one time at everything around him. Nothing looked unusual, just the usual business that surrounded the area on a regular basis. People ran about here and there, to and from incoming trains. Feeling satisfied, he laid back and closed his eyes, propping both feet up on the dashboard. "Damn, I need to rest for like 10 minutes," he thought to himself.

Sergeant Cromier and three other special task force members sat in four unmarked cars that were positioned throughout the busy atmosphere. It was impossible for anyone to notice that they were police from where they sat and because their vehicles were unmarked.

From the minute the Blazer entered the parking lot, pictures were taken to capture every moment of the event as it went down, from beginning to end. Every aspect of the situation was being recorded nothing was being missed.

Approaching the Brentwood Road entrance, Born flicked on the right signal as he slowed the candy red Honda Accord to make the quick swoop around the bend. Cruising down the entrance strip, in the distance, he caught sight of the pretty blazer as it sat amongst other vehicles sitting stationary, standing out like a vehicle on the show room floor, polished to the tee. Driving up, Born noticed that the parking space next to Jasheem was empty so he directed the Honda into the empty parking space. As he got out of the car, he looked around as if to show Jasheem that he was being cautious. He did not know that Jasheem was in a deep sleep until he came to the passenger window. With a flick of the wrists, three times he knocked lightly, awaking his sleeping friend. Jasheem practically snapped his neck, jumping up out of subconscious thought, allowing a little bit of saliva to drip down his lip. Still not fully awake, he wiped at his mouth with his left hand, using the right to reach over and unlock the passenger door.

"What's the deal, god?" Born stated as he jumped into the car.

"Peace!" Jasheem replied, watching Born unzip both side pockets of his jacket and grabbing a hold of bundles of money, which made a crackling sound. He made sure to hold the money up to the windshield so that it would not be hard for 5-0 to get pictures of it. He even went as far as to unwrap the money in direct view, allowing the beasts to catch a glimpse of everything.

Jasheem was totally ignorant to what was going down, and plus he was exhausted and showed every bit of it in his face and sluggish body movement. More than anything, he just wanted to get the deal over with so that he could bounce, go home, and catch some zzz's. H trusted this childhood friend with his life, so there was no need to recount the stash. Without saying a word, he reached under the seat below him and pulled out a medium-sized brown paper bag placing it on top of Born's lap.

Born's adrenaline started to rush once Jasheem placed the bag on his lap because the reality of what was taking place finally set in, and he was truly sorry. The long arm of the law wanted someone, and someone they would get. But it would not be him, he rationalized, in this case, friendship meant nothing. There was nothing else to think about, the deal was done. Grabbing a hold of the bag without looking into it, he smiled at Jasheem, nothing sinister, just a regular smile. "Tap me on my pager." Jasheem stated, giving Born a pound before starting the truck up.

"No doubt, god" Born replied, sliding out of the passenger side with the bag palmed in his right hand as if it contained a box or a forty ounce of malt liquor.

Leaving smoke fumes in its wake, the Blazer was out of sight within a matter of mere seconds, before Born even got in the Accord and bounced. His destination was already planned a day ahead.

*   *   *   *   *

Sitting along a bench in the Foot Locker sportswear store in South Shore Mall, Blaze waited on this young, pretty oriental store clerk to bring him back a pair of kicks from the storage room out back. Looking around as he sat waiting, he glanced at all the people who passed by. For some reason, the mall seemed to be extra busy with activity for a Tuesday afternoon. Not that he minded at all, in fact, he especially took notice of all the young ladies who passed the store front, causing him to look their way wide-eyed. Some eyed him as well, smiling and giving him the look over. It was all in fun though because he dated rarely and thought about Rachel all the time. She was his soul mate and he knew that someday they'd be together once again. For now he had to do what he had to do. She'd wait for him; this he had no doubt in his mind about whatsoever.

Caught up in the rapture of his thoughts, he was awoke out of the trance by a very soft tap on the left shoulder. Turning around instantly Blaze, was eye to eye with the beautiful young lady holding a box with the words Reebok written on the top. As he smiled back at her, she placed the box on the floor of his feet.

"Thank you," he said smirking.

Shyly before walking off, she replied, "You're welcome. If you need anything else, call me." With that she bounced off toward another customer. He could see that she was blushing a little even though he knew she tried her hardest to conceal it. Her small figure gracefully moved in very soft strides, mesmerizing him as he bent over to try on the new footwear. His pager went off. With a quick snatch from its casing and pressing the first of three buttons he realized it was his attorney. Without hesitation he threw the sneakers he came in with back on and raced up to the counter with the box.

"Is there anything else you want?" the attendant asked, sensing that Blaze was in a rush.

Still holding the Motorola he stated, "Nah," and pulled out a huge bankroll peeling off a one hundred dollar bill and then a fifty, handing it to the frail older woman behind the counter. She had this snotty look about her, but he didn't mind because he was in a rush anyway. Taking the change, he turned on his heels almost in a run. Speeding toward the front past the other customers he said goodbye to the young oriental lady who was eyeing him as she helped another customer. Smiling in return, she waved back.

Racing to the phone booth near the mall's main entrance, he threw the Foot Locker bag to the floor and began dialing. After the third ring, someone picked up. "Mr. Raynes' office, who's speaking?" a female secretary asked.

Practically cutting into her sentence, he replied, "Jermaine Johnson, Mr. Raynes just paged me."

"Oh, okay, Mr. Johnson, hold on one moment while I click you over to Mr. Raynes' line, okay?"

He waited, wondering what the attorney could possibly want. Two seconds later, Mr. Raynes was on the other end.

"Hey, Jermaine how are you doing?" he asked happily.

"I'm okay," Blaze stated quickly.

"I have some good news for you. They dropped all the cases against you. All they want you to plead to is a disorderly conduct charge which is nothing but a violation." Before Blaze could say anything, Mr. Raynes interjected, "Your sentence date is in six weeks, November eighth at 1:00 PM in room D34 in Central Islip court. Don't be late, okay, I gotta go cuz I have someone else on the other line waiting, alright?" He hung up the phone abruptly, leaving Blaze with a dial tone. Had it been any other day, he would have been pissed, but at the moment he felt like screaming and jumping with joy. A smirk covered his face like Indian paint as he leaned over to pick up the Foot Locker bag and stepped toward the exit.

"Looks like there is light at the end of the tunnel" he thought to himself.

Chapter Thirteen

T he day was a glorious one for District Attorney Patters, ever since he received permission from the Honorable Judge S. Madison to place wire taps on the phones of all suspected brotherhood members and affiliates. In the process, maybe they'd get lucky and become aware of other criminal activities the group was involved in.

The night before had to have been one of the district attorney's happiest. It couldn't get any better for him to find out that there was a significant break through in the Brotherhood case. One of their suspected members had made a sale of a large amount of cocaine to an informant. The best thing about this was that it was all caught on film. How better could it get? He was so happy that he could have kissed Sergeant Cromier through the phone. He was excited to say the least. The man's milky white complexion was red with laughter and joy as he talked to the sergeant. This case represented the best opportunity of his career to really make his name known. And it could not have come at a better time because it was no secret to anyone who knew him that he had his eyes set on running for some type of political office. The bottom line was that he aspired for social standing and success, and would use or step on whomever he had to achieve his goals. To him, every situation was nothing but an opportunity for growth or stagnation. It was all about what choice you wanted to make. This is the type of talk he would always shoot at his subordinate, assistant district attorneys whenever they were presented with a new case.

Sergeant Cromier had done his job well. Now it was only a matter of time before the whole case came together. With the secret indictment already secured against Jasheem, the authorities had time and the element of surprise on their side. Now it was all a matter of seeing how many fish they could trap before bringing the net back in. For now, they would have to sit, lay a few more traps, and wait.

*   *   *   *   *

The sound of an alarm clock was all that could be heard throughout the small bedroom before awaking its owner out of a comatose sleep. He was in one of those, drinking the night before sleeps, practically everyone experiences at least one time in their life.

Sliding the blanket over, Freedom reached over, grabbing a hold of the phone and pulling it up under the covers with him.

"Yo! What's the deal?" he asked in a raspy voice.

"It's me, god, Jasheem. I'm a be out there in like a half an hour, ok?"

Freedom, almost fell asleep once again as he held the phone to his ear.

"Yo, wake up, god, I'm a be there in a few. So don't go the fuck back to sleep. Yo, we gotta bounce to Manhattan to see Papo before eleven cuz you know after that the beast is gonna be all around stressing cats. I'm not trying to get caught with all this shit. The situation uptown is mad hot." With that, Jasheem hung up the phone, feeling a bit frustrated because more than likely he would have to awaken his friend again. He knew Freedom well enough to know that by the time he hung up, he was back under the covers curled up. And he was absolutely right because Freedom crashed out as soon the phone receiver was placed in the cradle. His head was pounding, causing him to moan before diving back into unconsciousness.

Jasheem was out of the house toting a duffel bag, which he slung over his shoulder to the car. The sound of the car's alarm went off before he clicked it off, and then slid into the driver's seat and closed the door. The car's engine revved up as he pressed his foot on the gas and took off.

Jasheem hit Sunrise Highway and stepped on the gas pedal, accelerating the car to 90mph. The car felt like it was gliding as the air lifted under it. For the most part, the road ahead was clear except for an occasional vehicle here and there. This was great because he was able to take the vehicle in and out of lanes without braking or slowing down.

Ten minutes later, the sign for the Central Islip exit stood out in the distance. Seeing this, he released his foot from the gas pedal, slowly minimizing speed before hitting the exit ramp. Once around the bend and up onto Carlton Avenue, he took the car to a cool 40mph.

Ten minutes later, he was whipping the car into Freedom's driveway, beeping the horn three times before he came to a complete stop. After waiting a few minutes and seeing that his friend was not coming, he got out and strolled to the front door and rang the doorbell.

Freedom was somewhere between consciousness and sleep when he heard the sound of a car pulling into the driveway, sounding off the horn three times before quietness took over. He knew it was Jasheem, so with all his might, he rolled over, stumbling off the bed onto the carpet as the quilt rested halfway on the surface of the queen size bed, while the remainder rested on the carpet.

The doorbell chimed three times. "Hold on, god!" he managed to scream out as he stomped to the door heavily.

Unlocking and then yanking the door open quickly, Freedom almost fell to the ground as the sunlight rushed into his eyes. At once, he lifted his right arm up to his face to block the suns rays on his eyes. Pulling the screen door open, Jasheem stormed in, almost knocking his friend to the floor by accident. "I'm a go get the horn to page Papo and let him know that we're gonna be around in like an hour." Without saying anything else, he strolled into the kitchen, throwing the backpack on top of the counter and causing a shrieking thud as it hit the surface. Grabbing the phone he dialed Papo's pager, leaving an area code 516 and then Freedoms number. By the time he turned around to say something to Freedom, he heard the shower water running.

Picking up a glass from the countertop, Jasheem walked over to rinse it out before going into the refrigerator and looking to see what was there to drink. A half-gallon carton of Tropicana orange juice was the first thing he noticed because it stood out on the top shelf. Orange juice was his favorite beverage, so seeing the carton brought a smile and eager thirst.

Carrying the glass of orange juice into the living room, he turned on the TV and sat down to wait on his friend. Since the shower was no longer running, he knew that it would not be long before they were on their way. The Simpsons cartoon played on the screen, and he laughed for the next ten minutes until Freedom called out to him from the kitchen.

"Yo, god, how many are you gonna get? I'm getting two." Jasheem could hear the sound of money being counted before he even walked into the kitchen to reply.

"I'm getting two too, my thirty-four is in the knapsack. There's two more zip-lock bags in there so you can put yours in there too."

At once, Freedom stacked the one hundred dollar big faces into thousand dollar stacks. As soon as this was completed, he then placed seventeen thousand in each bag before placing both full bags back in the knapsack along with the other thirty-four thousand. Jasheem watched on without saying anything. Instead, he sipped on the glass of orange juice like it was exquisite liquor, savoring every bit of it.

"Let's get out of here." Freedom stated as he walked back toward his room. Jasheem did not need to be told twice. As a matter of fact, he already held the knapsack and was trooping out the door.

As Freedom reached the front door, he could hear the sound of the cars engine blowing mildly as the ignition kicked in. Slamming the door and then locking it behind him, he leaped down the stoop, half-jogging toward the car and then sliding in. As he fixed the seat to lean back, he turned his head toward his partner, "Let's stop at 7-11, and then get some gas."

Jasheem already had the gear snatched into reverse and was backing up out of the driveway before responding.

"Yeah, that's what I was gonna do anyway cuz my stomach is touching my back right about now."

After placing in a mix tape, Freedom closed his eyes and concentrated on the future and the day's events.

Jasheem was also in deep thought about the day ahead. The thought of money took away his headache and gave him a clear outlook. As he drove, he observed everything around him with a keen eye. At the speed they were going, if they did not hit any real traffic, they would be at their destination in about forty-five minutes.

* * * * *

Papo was up, which was nothing unusual because he always awoke early to make sure that all his drug spots had enough product to open up. He had three spots, the main one which he oversaw on 158th and Amsterdam, one on 139th and Amsterdam, and another on 145th and Broadway, which was a telecommunications business providing long distance phone service mainly to Hispanic immigrants seeking to reach people in their native countries.

Once he saw the 516 page in his pager with a phone number and a four behind it, he knew that Jasheem wanted four kilos. At the moment the pager went off, he was busy having sex with his wife. She threw a fit, but to no avail because he jumped off of her quickly to call the number back. He did not get an answer, and the phone just kept on ringing, but he didn't worry because, he knew that they were on their way to see him. The situation was pre-planned the night before. So there was no need for them to have bothered paging him. He was already on point.

Since the two always came to the main spot on 158th, there was not a long wait since the stash was kept somewhere nearby in the neighborhood. The wait was never more than ten or fifteen minutes.

About fifty minutes after their initial departure from Long Island, they were now at the stop light on 155th street and Saint Nicholas waiting for the light to turn green so they could make the right towards 158th street.

Once the light turned green, Jasheem cut a quick right taking the car up into Washington Heights. Nudging Freedom hard, he stated, "Gee, get up, we're here."

Jasheem practically jumped up out of the seat, rubbing his face with both hands, looking around. It looked as if he was paranoid. But this was not the case at all, in fact, he always behaved like this, he was just the observant type.

"It's better to be aware of your surroundings and what you're dealing with than unaware and then surprised by an unfavorable situation. These are the words his father would always tell him as a youngster, when he took up a class in martial arts because other kids in school had him under pressure.

Whipping the car around 158th and Covenant, the block before Amsterdam, Freedom immediately looked for a parking space, but could not find one. As a result, he decided to take the car up to Amsterdam. Usually, he would have decided against it, but since it was so early in the morning, it really didn't matter because the streets were practically empty. As he approached the block, he could see that only two people were on the block, Hector and some other young cat. Hector flagged them once he saw their car.

In front of the seven-story building, Freedom parked the car while Jasheem grabbed the knapsack and pulled out his .380 semi-automatic, stuffing it into the front waistline of his pants. Giving each other the nod, they both stepped out of the car together, without saying anything. Hector smiled, stating, "Papo's upstairs." before either of them could ask.

Jasheem paid him no mind, while Freedom gave the young soldier a peace sign as he followed in step behind Jasheem into the building. Entering the corridor they were greeted by one of the security members of Papo's team who buzzed them into the main door.

Taking seven flights of steps at a jogging pace caused them both to breathe a little more heavily than usual as they reached the last floor. Looking behind him to make sure Freedom was behind him, Jasheem smirked at his partner before knocking on apartment 7B. Inside the apartment, footsteps could be heard approaching from behind the door. Someone looked through the peephole as they pressed their body against the door. The lock clicked, and then the chain rattled before the door opened. Freddie, Papo's lieutenant stood there smiling, "Hey, my compadres!" he stated as they breezed past him, each of them patting him on the shoulder before seeking the kitchen, where Papo was sitting on a chair behind a small glass table calculating the figures in a book.

Anytime anyone purchased material from the spot, no matter how big or small the amount it was calculated in a book used to figure out the earnings almost like what an account does.

Once they both entered the kitchen, Papo got up and hugged them before telling them to take a seat with him. While Papo went back to what he was doing, Jasheem and Freedom placed all the money on top of the counter, recounting and stacking it once again in thousand dollar piles. This only took about five minutes or so. While they did this, Papo didn't once take his eyes off what he was doing to look up at them or the money until about three minutes after they were finished.

"Everything straight?" Papo asked, looking at Jasheem and then Freedom.

"Yeah, it's all good. We still want the four girls." Freedom replied, crossing both of his hands together and smiling at their Latin associate, handing him the car keys.

Getting up from the seat, Papo said, "Where's the car parked?"

Immediately Jasheem replied, "Right out in front of the building."

Papo started to walk towards the door.

"Give me ten minutes," he stated before walking out the door, telling his lieutenant "Get them something to drink, Freddy, I'll be right back."

He walked out, slamming the door behind him as Freddie came behind him, locking both locks.

Trotting down the flights of stairs, Papo reached the bottom. The security at the first door buzzed him out and stepped out in back of him while he walked out onto the pavement, handing the keys to Hector.

The young, obedient soldier got in the car and started up the ignition while Papo looked on. There was no need for him to say anything, because this situation was a regular occurrence. Pulling off the curb, Hector took the car to Broadway, making a right and disappearing around the corner. Seeing this, Papo walked across the street into the next building.

Ten minutes later, Hector pulled up and parked the car in the exact spot he moved it from. Beeping the horn two times, he pulled the keys from the ignition and jumped out, waiting for his boss to come out of the building.

"Alright?" Papo asked the young hustler who was standing in front of him wide-eyed and happy that he completed the task given to him. Hector was so delighted that he almost forgot about the car keys.

Laughing, he said "Oh here!" chucking the keys across the air to Papo, who caught them with one swift motion.

"Come with me, Hector" Papo ordered, walking across the street without looking back. He stepped onto the steps, pushing the heavy steel door open and walking to the next one. Security buzzed him back in and the two walked back up the steps at a fast pace. Papo tapped the apartment door with his knuckles six times.

Freddie was deep into watching a Spanish soap opera when he heard the six taps. He jumped up from the sofa and stepped to the door. Looking through the peephole for a split second, he could see Papo's face as his hands held fast on the locks. "Click, click, click," the sound of the door unlocking was the only noise that could be heard. Papo and Hector walked through the narrow doorway, stepping right into the kitchen where Freedom and Jasheem waited along with the stack of one hundred dollar big faces. Sitting down at the table while Hector stood in back of him, Papo began to count the stacks placing the bills in five thousand dollar piles. While he did this he remained silent until every bill was accounted for. As a matter of fact, there was one extra hundred-dollar bill, which he pushed aside toward Jasheem.

"Sixty eight thousand," he mumbled to no one in particular after counting the last stack. Looking at the two, he smiled, yet it was not because of the money in front of him, it was because of the friendship that was built between them throughout the years of doing business together. He was a millionaire; sixty eight thousand was nothing for him to get excited about.

"The cars out front?" Freedom asked as Jasheem got up. Papo was wrapping the stacks of money with rubber bands and placing each one inside a garbage bag. Without stopping, he looked up.

"Right out in front. It's all taken care of, Papi."

With that, Jasheem and Freedom hugged the smaller man as he got up. Once Freddie opened the door for them, they exited as if they were trying to escape. Everything else was a flash, and before the two realized it, they were back at the tolls on the Throgs Neck Bridge on their way back to Long Island. This time, Jasheem drove while Freedom passed out on the passenger side. Even the blasting system failed to keep him awake. Freedom, on the other hand, was wide-awake, and dodged in and out of lanes carefully and looked in the rearview and side mirrors for police every now and then. "This is the price you pay in the game," he thought as he drove on a little nervously.

About twenty minutes after the car entered the boundaries of Nassau County, Freedom's cellular phone rang. Palming the large phone, which resembled a walkie-talkie with one hand, he pressed send. "What's the deal?" he mouthed into the receiver.

"This is Blaze, god, where you at?"

Looking ahead at the signs, Freedom stated, "We're in Nassau about to come home. We just came back, gee. The god is over here asleep next to me."

"Alright, gee, when y'all touch down, tap me on my pager" Blaze mentioned.

"Peace!" Freedom replied as the other line clicked off.

Chapter Fourteen

"Is Messiah home?"

His brother answered, "Yeah, what's this?"

The thing, which bugged Blaze with this kid, was that as often as the kid heard Blaze's voice, he would still ask who it was as if he had no clue. So with a little conviction and attitude Blaze answered, "Blaze!"

The kid did not reply, instead, he got off the phone and a few seconds later, Messiah picked up, "Yeah, what's up?" Blaze asked.

Messiah said, "Come over to the apartment at three o'clock." The reason this arrangement was made was because his house was hot and was constantly being watched by detectives. And from out the gate, he told Blaze months ago that his phone line might be tapped. So it was no necessary to be very careful and not speak too much or say anything incriminating.

Messiah was one of Blaze's customers, he sold product on the street level. Blaze was just one step above him, and supplied the street dealers. In other words, if they came to him with fifty, he would give them enough product to double their money. Now the more money they brought to him the more he would give them in exchange, enabling them to make more of a profit. Blaze liked this arrangement because; it kind of put him out of harms reach. It was definitely better than sticking up, and always having to watch his back out of fear that someone was coming to get him.

Any criminal knows that there is no safety within the confines of the criminal world. But the bottom line was that Blaze knew he was much more protected than Messiah. The streets are the battlefields, and the street corner hustlers were the front line soldiers. No one could be trusted. Crack heads will turn on anyone just so they can remain on the streets and get high. It's not unusual for the beast to give an addict marked money to buy some drugs from a dealer. Then there were also cases where under cover police pretended to be crack heads, so they could cop some drugs and then make the bust.

Blaze was fully aware of the pros and cons of the situation. He learned them coming up in the game and being a participant. One thing he realized that others didn't was that the key to making money was having discipline and being able to manage your money. The object is for one to make more money than they spend, and always have money making money.

Blaze's situation had its down points too because dealers are known to set other dealers up as well. This is street politics at its finest. One thing was for sure; Blaze did not trust Messiah at all. Yet he knew that life every minute of the day was a gamble when you hustled. He was a player of both games, so chances had to be taken.

After thinking back on the events of that day, for some reason, he did not feel like conducting any business at all that day. It was just one of those gut feelings he had that told him to stay home, and this is exactly what he planned to do. Plus, Rachel was hounding him to spend time together, and he felt it was due for him to lie up, chill and give her some quality time. Especially, they just smoothed things out and were back together.

*   *   *   *   *

Down in the bedroom room, Rachel and he lay along the bed. "I'll be right back," he tells her. Leaving the room he runs upstairs into the kitchen. His mind was racing with thoughts so fast that he could barely decipher them. While this was going on in his head he knew his main focus was to grab a can of fruit from the cupboard. Looking in the cabinet he saw that there is no fruit cocktail, only pineapples and peaches. "Hmm, pineapples" he decides. Satisfied with this thought, he opens the can by with an electric can opener. Placing the fruit in a tall glass, he smirked, smiling all the way back downstairs.

As he walked into the room, Rachel raised her head from the pillow to look at him "Go, get out of here. I hate you!" she stated, laughing.

He was all smiles because it really felt good to be there with her this moment.

"Are you sure you want to do this?" he asked her with a devious grin.

"Boy, stop playing" she replied, staring into his eyes.

Without replying back he began to kiss her, drawing her close to him. The coming off of the clothes was in such a rhythm that it was like a slow sensual dance. Laying her naked body down, he sat in between her legs. Then he took a slice of pineapple and wiped it all over her breasts and stomach and began to kiss and suck the juice. Doing her inner thighs, legs, and feet caused her to gasp out loud in pleasure. He had to think about it, but he decided that he was going to hold no punches and give her the pleasure of her life. "I might as well," he though to himself. Taking a pineapple slice, he began to rub it around the surface of her vagina, and in and around her clitoris. Parting he legs wide apart, he started to lick around her vagina lips before sticking his tongue into the depths of her.

Entering her with a deep thrust, he caused her to gasp and place her hands toward his chest to ease the penetration. It didn't help because he moved her hands and held them as he plowed into her deeper. As he felt himself about to release, he grabbed her buttocks and held her tightly to him, enjoying the sensation that overcame him as the hot liquid shot into her and caused them both to moan in ecstasy.

For about ten minutes, they both laid exhausted, absorbing each other's sweat. Neither of them spoke, instead they listened to one another's breathing and heart rhythms. Minutes later, they fell asleep in each other's arms.

When Blaze awoke, the first thing that he noticed was the noise that has pager was making along the surface of the dresser. Moving Rachel's arm from around his waist, he pulled the covers over her and got up quietly. Pressing forward button on his pager, he calculated that he had about ten pages waiting, totaling about twelve hundred dollars.

He was torn between going out and getting that money and just allowing it fly by and letting tomorrow be another day. Rachel was asleep, so she wasn't going anywhere. Plus, he rationalized that he'd have the business handled before she even got up and noticed he was gone.

"Fuck it! I gotta get this doe," he told himself as he got dressed, and at the same time he paged his boy Omar, who would drive him around from time to time because he had a valid driver's license.

About ten minutes later, the phone rang. Not letting it ring more than once, Blaze asked, "Who's speaking?"

"Yo, what's the deal?" was the reply on the other end.

"Nothing much, gee, we have to stop by to see Messiah" stated Blaze.

"I'll be there in twenty minutes," Omar said before hanging up. And true to his word, twenty-five minutes later, the doorbell rang. Walking towards the front door, Blaze yelled, "Come in, sun!"

"What's up? You ready?" Omar asked.

"Yeah, let's bounce" Blaze replied, walking out the door.

Omar had a Range Rover that he bought used for thirty thousand. And as they drove, Blaze noticed right away how smoothly the vehicle rode, even though it was a SUV. Coming onto Messiah's block Blaze reminded Omar to park in the parking lot of the apartment complex two addresses away from Messiah's house.

Looking around for any unusual vehicles or police, Blaze decided that it was ok to get out. Strolling out the car in a fast step, he walked over to the side of Messiah's house, which was where the entrance was to his apartment. Approaching the screen door, Blaze noticed that it was closed shut. After knocking for about two minutes, he decided to step back to the car. After all, Messiah paged him at three and he was there three and a half hours late. So it was a hit or miss situation that he'd be there in the first place.

Once Blaze stepped in the car Omar asked "Was he there?"

"Nah, he must have bounced after waiting for so long cuz he did page me at three. But, fuck it, he'll probably call me later."

"Yo, I have to go to Blockbuster to turn these movies in, and get some more before we shoot to the center to see that kid."

Everything was cool for the first couple of miles away from Messiah's house. But as Blaze and Omar approached Blockbuster, they could hear sirens behind them. Blaze had already had a brush up with the law, so his first instinct was to look for a blue and white marked police vehicle. He did not see one, but then it dawned on him that it was the rust colored Celebrity with plain clothes, tailing the Range Rover. "Oh, shit!" was Blaze's first reaction. He had an ounce of rock in the pocket of his sweat pants. The first thought that came to him was to stuff it under the seat, yet he realized that the detectives would see him making this movement. And from past experiences, he knew they were going to search the truck anyway. Plus, if they found it in the truck then they would charge both of them with it, which is something that Blaze did not want. Omar could not go down for his stuff, he decided. Regardless of what happened, Blaze knew the charge could be beat because, neither him nor Omar had any warrants. Omar had a valid driver's license, so there was no reason for the police to search them or the truck. Anything found in such an instance, would fall under the statue of law covering "illegal search and seizure."

To Blaze, the scene seemed just like a movie, and he knew today the ending was not going to be good. There were two detectives who approached the car, one on either side, a black officer and a white one. The black detective approached Blaze's side while the white one stepped to Omar's.

As the white detective approached Omar's side, Omar pressed the switch to roll down the window. "Can I see your license and registration?" the detective asked. Handing him his license, he reached over to the glove compartment and retrieved the registration. After receiving both, the detective backed away, heading to the celebrity to run everything in.

As he was busy doing this, the black detective asked Blaze, "What's your name?"

"Jermaine Johnson" Blaze replied.

"Do you have any warrants?" the detective questioned.

"Nah" Blaze answered a bit irritated by the question.

"Let me see some identification, Mr. Johnson" the detective asked. And as Blaze passed him I.D., the detective asked him if he could search him. To this Blaze said "No, I have I.D., so why do you want to search me?"

With a smirk the detective said, "Step out of the car." and placed his right hand over the Glocks holster-fastened to his waist. Blaze knew that he was holding so he was hoping that he could play the detective mentally. So he stated, "Y'all don't have anything to do but harass people for nothing."

Before he could go further, the white detective stated, "If you don't get out the car there are gonna be problems."

At this moment, the black detective opened the door pulling Blaze out, saying, "Oh, you don't have your track sneakers on today. Place your hands on top of the car."

The only thing which was on Blaze's mind at that moment was how he was gonna sprint on this cop, so that he could at least get rid of this product. But there seemed to be no way out because they were along a main busy road and there was no where to run. Plus, the whole strip was filled with stores. If this were the hood he thought, he'd definitely be leaving this cat in the dust. The only things they would see were his arms and the bottoms of his sneakers in the distance.

Reaching into Blaze's right pocket the detective pulled out a clear bag with packages of crack cocaine in it. Throwing the bag on the seat, the detective grabbed Blaze's hands, placing them behind his back.

"What a fucking nightmare," Blaze thought to himself while being handcuffed.

Taking Blaze to the Celebrity the detective asked, "Does this guy have anything on him?"

"Nah, he doesn't have anything to do with this." Blaze answered.

Sitting in the back of the Celebrity, Blaze could see the detectives asking Omar questions. He motioned for his friend not to say anything.

As it turned out, Omar was handcuffed as well. But instead of being placed in the Celebrity alongside Blaze, he was put in a blue and white patrol car.

Before Blaze could see what else was going on, he was being driven to the 5th precinct. On the way there, the detective turned to Blaze and stated, "Listen, you know we can work something out. What are you doing, supplying Messiah? Looks like you are doing well for yourself. And plus, no one out there is trying to go to jail, so why should you? Just help us out, and we'll see about you making precinct bail." Blaze wanted to laugh at the asshole. The beast was talking like it was a simple 1-2-3 situation. Give someone up and then they'll let him go. Then they'll want him to finger people in trials. Or go set people up in person. Was this guy stupid, or crazy? Maybe he was a little of both.

Blaze was nowhere near the biggest dealer out there, yet he was fully aware of the pros and cons of doing time. The bottom-line was that if you do crime you take a chance of getting caught and doing some time.

While the detective spoke to him, Blaze kept his gaze in the opposite direction, looking at the scenery outside the window.

"I hate cops, and snitches, so why should I help you?" were the words Blaze felt like saying. Instead, he decided to not talk at all. What sense did it make anyway? It wasn't going to get him out of the handcuffs. Instead, it might get him an ass whooping. The 5th precinct detectives were infamous for getting down and dirty like that.

Blaze did not know whether to laugh or cry. Here it was this beast was bringing reality straight to him. Telling him in so many words that there were two roads for him to take. One was to freedom and the other was to incarceration. But what about honor? And then again, is there really honor amongst thieves? Or is it just a slick saying "death before dishonor." Either way, Blaze was not going to sacrifice his manhood or principles. What type of man would he be? He asked himself. Fuck the world and what everyone else thought about him. It's about what he would think of himself. That's what it's all about, respect for self.

The ride to the precinct was only about three miles, yet it seemed like it took a half hour to get there. Thoughts of the first time he got arrested came to him, and how he got off so easily. For some reason, he just knew that this time was going to be a little different. His intuition told him so.

The weird thing about it all was that in the precinct the detectives did not put him through any hassle at all; instead, they processed him quickly, taking his fingerprints and filling out the necessary paperwork. Once this was done, he was taken into a different room and strip frisked before being placed in a cell. The only things he was allowed to wear were his sweat pants, t-shirt, boxers, and his socks. All other belongings were placed into a property bag and thrown into a bin with each prisoner's cell number written on it.

It took Blaze about an hour to go to sleep because of the cold atmosphere in the holding pen. And when he finally did doze off, it was a very uncomfortable light sleep. One thing was for sure, there definitely was not going to be any pleasant dreams this night. Neither would he be able to sleep straight through it comfortably, without waking up a few times in the middle of the night.

*   *   *   *   *

Two weeks after Blaze's initial arrest for possession in the 3rd degree of an uncontrolled substance, he was once again taken to court and arraigned, this time for the charge of conspiracy to distribute and sell an uncontrolled substance.

He found out after being locked up for the second day that Jasheem, Papo, and thirteen other members of the team were arrested on conspiracy charges. It had to do with the phone lines being tapped. Freedom was the only one who escaped, and he was now on the run. Each passing day Blaze waited with agony for them to get him from his cell. And two weeks later, it happened.

The bullpen area was busy; sheriffs and legal aide attorneys ran around like crazy from one holding area to another. Blaze was oblivious to all this though, because his mind was full of all types of different thoughts. There were about eight other cats inside the bullpen. He did not know any of them, and didn't want to know any of them. So he talked to no one. Nothing mattered until he heard a voice call out "Johnson!"

Staring up at the bars, as he sat on the bench and heard his name, he stepped toward the gate saying, "Right here."

Once he stated this, the deputy opened the gate motioning him to step forward and stating, "When you step out, step to the right and face the bars, placing both hands in back of you." Blaze said nothing and followed the deputy's orders as the handcuffs were placed around his wrists.

"You have an attorney visit," the deputy stated to him as he directed Blaze to walk forward. Faces of all shades looked at him through the bars as he passed each holding pen. He was not in the mood, so he didn't bother to look at the many faces that recognized him. Some even called out his name while he was being ushered down the hallway.

The deputy brought Blaze to an area where there were five or six individual cubicles. On one side stood attorneys, and on the other stood prisoners. Mr. Raynes was already present when Blaze arrived. To say the least, the man did not look too happy today at all, and he showed it in every way. Usually, he would smile once he saw Blaze, but today was different; instead, he gave Blaze a serious, solemn look as if he was contemplating very hard about something. Looking up from his book of notes and documents he spoke, "As I'm sure you are aware of, some of your friends have been arrested for conspiracy. From the information that I have, the suspect made a 500gram sale to a police informant two and a half months ago. Once this was done the district attorney was given permission to tap his phone and anyone who was thought to be affiliated with any dealings he was involved in. So that means that everyone who called him, and who seemed to have a very close in relationship with him, as well as those who talked very suspiciously, their phones were tapped as well. As a result of being in phone contact with him, you fell in the picture because you made a phone call to someone in Manhattan by the name of Papo. Papo is a known drug dealer, big time, and he has a past criminal record to show for it. The district attorney right now is hinting at a four to life sentence. Everyone is getting fiver years and better. They seem to be very determined not to let up on this situation. From what I hear, this new investigation was a byproduct of the one they had involving the cases that were dismissed against you a while back. He specifically stated that he was not going to come down from a four to life for you." Pausing for a moment, he took his eyes off Blaze and once again began shuffling through his papers. Shaking his head from side to side, he sucked on his teeth and looked up at Blaze. "Call me tomorrow at three, and I'll know for sure what they have, and then we can go from there."

Blaze was too dazed to say anything besides, "Alright."

As Attorney Raynes packed up his gear, Blaze eyed him closely, wondering whether to trust the man or not. "Never trust no one," sounded off his in his head.

"I want to see documentation of the phone conversation, Mr. Raynes." Blaze stated loud enough so the attorney could hear even as he began to walk away from the conference area.

Turning around the attorney stated, "Okay, just call me tomorrow and we'll discuss everything." With these words, he disappeared through a door leaving Blaze standing in handcuffs by himself.

Five minutes later, a deputy came to him asking, "Are you ready to go?"

"Yeah," Blaze stated feeling a bit uncomfortable and irritated. As he walked away with the deputy on the side of him, he wondered how he was going get out of the situation. A four to life did not sound good to him at all. What was going to happen to

Rachel and him? Was she going to wait or what? One thing was for sure, he was not going to tell her anything negative until he was sure of the situation. His mind was so boggled with conflicting thoughts that the deputy had to tell him two times to stop at the second holding pen before he recognized what the man was saying to him.

Once Blaze entered the pen, he walked directly to the bench on the right hand side, finding some room toward the back and sat in a slouched position with the palms of both hands covering his face. Before he knew it, he was fast asleep, in another zone, unaware of the chaos that was taking place everywhere as prisoners, lawyers, and deputies occupied the cramped bullpen area.

The rattling of chains awakened him, and once he came to his senses, he realized that it was time to go back to Riverhead jail. The chains reminded him of the movie "Roots" and as he looked at the deputies, he wondered whether they received joy out of doing what they were doing. It was like they were the slave keepers, taking the slaves back to the plantation.

Each chain held four sets of handcuffs, which enabled the deputies to chain up four prisoners at once. As all the prisoners were cuffed, one by one, each bullpen was emptied.

In groups of eight the prisoners were herded outside to waiting deputies and buses. Inside, the buses had enough room to sit twenty-four bodies. It was crazy to Blaze how it seemed that most of the guys did not seem bothered by being shackled like cattle. They chatted and talked about everything under the sun freely. He felt like telling each and every one of them to "shut the fuck up!" But he quickly thought against it because there were just too many of them. For a minute, as he watched the deputy seated behind the gate, he even dreamed of grabbing the guy's gun and making a run for it. Realistically, this could not happen with handcuffs, he rationalized. So he went to rest, nodding, but waking up every time the bus came to an abrupt stop or hit a bump in the road.

About twenty minutes, later the bus arrived in Riverhead. "This is home for now," Blaze thought silently, as the bus pulled up to the gate. All that was left was the process of being unhand cuffed, pat frisked, and then taken back upstairs to the tier 4, west north. Life could not get any worse.

Walking onto the gallery, the C.O. asked him his name before opening the cell area and letting him in. Strolling through the area, which had about twenty cells, as he walked down to his cell, he had to walk past everyone on that side of the gallery because they were watching a movie in the front.

Blaze was a recognized hood figure, so he knew many of the brothers who were locked up with him. Those he did not know knew of him. Most of them took notice of his presence as he entered the area. But no one spoke to him because it was evident by the look on his face that he was deep in thought. To be perfectly honest, he was not in the mood to speak anyway. He walked by, entered his dreary cell, and threw himself on the bed without undressing.

He managed to sleep all the way through to the next morning without awaking for anything. His dreams were long and endless, as his mind searched his soul for answers to what lay ahead for him. When he awoke, it was because one of the brothers on the gallery tapped him on the shoulder to see if he was going to eat breakfast. Waking with slob dripping from his mouth, he mumbled "Yeah?"

"Come on brother, its breakfast time" the older man stated. Blaze looked around the cell and at the old man, confused because he wondered how was it that he was able to sleep the whole night through without waking up at least once. Looking at himself he realized that he was wearing everything except for his sneakers. Turning toward the old man once again, he stated, "Ok, I'll be there in a minute." The old man smiled, causing his white teeth to blend in with the shade of his salt and pepper colored hair. Feeling satisfied with the young man's reply, he turned around and left without saying another word.

For some reason, Blaze's body felt sore, and as he stretched, sharp pains shot through him. He moaned and exhaled getting up out of the bed.

After brushing his teeth and washing his face, he was ready to chow down on some breakfast. The food cart started to make its way down the gallery. The cart server stopped at every feed up slot on the gallery, distributing the morning's breakfast. A half pint of milk, two small boxes of cocoa crisps and an orange was the meal. This was just enough to tease a grown man. All the jail was concerned about was giving a prisoner the prescribed 2,000-calorie diet, which the health department mandates as the daily amount of calories needed for the average person to maintain a healthy diet.

Blaze took the little bit of food and bounced away from everyone to the confines of his cell. Thinking that he was alone, he was surprised to see that as he dumped the breakfast on the bed and turned around, the old man who awoke him stood in the doorway.

"What's going on, young brother?" the old man asked with his arms folded in front of him comfortably.

Sitting on the surface of the bed, Blaze looked at the man intently before stating, "Ain't nothing, pops, just the same shit."

"Yeah, I know how it is young blood but you got to hang in there." Smiling he went on, "Well, you know that already. You can't let this situation stress you out, this is what it is designed to do. You'll be all right though. You don't look like the average young knucklehead that comes through. And from what I read about y'all in yesterday's paper, it seems you cats were doing your thing. You just have to do your time and use it to get yourself together and decide what you want. This situation for the rest of your life, or freedom, it is that simple." Pointing at the pictures of Rachel that Blaze was standing in front of, he went on, "You have a pretty young lady there, and from what I see it seems like she is a real trooper as well. But, how much shit can you put her through before she's had enough. A lot of you cats got it misunderstood. Yeah, these days a lot of our young women are attracted to hustlers, but not for the reasons you think at all." Pointing his right index finger at Blaze he went on, "They like the hustler because they have that get up and get attitude. Yet, at the same time, they are quietly hoping that they can convince you to go out and get by legal means. If you put the same effort into the legal route as you do doing the illegal thing, then there's no reason why you should not be victorious. The only limitations that a man has are the ones he places on himself." Without saying anything else, the man backed out of Blaze's cell and walked away as quickly as he came.

Blaze was dazed by the old man's words of wisdom. So much so that he wanted to break down and cry. His pride would not let him go that far though. Plus, he knew it would do no good. He wondered what Rachel was thinking at that moment. Laying back on the bed, and kicking his sneakers off, he placed both palms on the top of his head.

"Why, when things are going good, does something always seems to happen?" he wondered to himself as he gazed at the cell's ceiling until he fell asleep.

Three hours later, he was woke to the sound of something pounding the cell's bars hard, then the sounds of many voices drowned out the banging. A fight was taking place. "Fuck 'em up, yo" Blaze heard, as he got up to walk out of his cell to see what was happening down the gallery. Blaze didn't to bother walk down into the crowd, but from what he saw, two brothers were brawling something fierce while the crowd cheered them on. He and the old man were the only ones who kept their distance.

Looking ahead at the crowd, the old man shook his head and snickered in disgust before looking at Blaze, who had already turned his head toward the older man observing his every facial movement.

"You see these assholes, they act like kids. This is why we're in the situation we're in. Grown men do not want to take the responsibility to be men. Now, instead of one of these older guys intervening and telling them young cats to chill, they cheer them on as those cats try to kill one another."

Just as he was about to say something else, about five C.O.'s ran down the catwalk outside the cell area yelling, "break it up!" several times. As the group dispersed, one of the officers yelled at the two fighting, telling them to stop. Well, it was basically over because one guy was on top of the other, pounding his face in with his right fist, which was wrapped up in a sock. So he was the only one fighting by this time, and gladly stopped when the officer directed him to. Pulling the sock off his right fist he threw it to the floor and walked up the gallery to the sally port, which was a washing area near the cell gallery entrance. Everyone looked at him and then at his opponent who struggled to get up and holding his mouth as blood oozed from cracks in his lips.

Everyone was directed to go back to their cells for lock down until the situation was taken care of. This was the usual routine whenever a fight broke out. As they parted ways, the old man told Blaze.

"I'll see you in a couple of hours."

All the cells closed shut, locking once everyone on the gallery stepped inside their cells. For the most part, their tier remained quiet, except for a few of the guys who spoke about the scuffle, and laughed and joked about the situation. Blaze listened to them with neither disgust nor curiosity. It was just something to do.

Listening to the different conversations that took place around him caused Blaze to realize that he really needed to utilize his time better. Reaching under his mattress, he picked up the book that Rachel had brought him on a visit two days before called "Think and Grow Rich: A Black Choice." The title alone intrigued him enough to make him want to read the book. Turning over on his stomach, he placed the book in front of him and opened to page one.

*   *   *   *   *

The morning weather was brisk and the afternoon did not seem to get any better. Rachel had the chills ever since the early morning. She did not know if it was because of the weather or the fact that she was worried about Blaze. For some reason, she just had the feeling that he was not doing well. Or was it just that she missed him so much? Looking in the rearview mirror as she approached the jail entrance she thought, "Shit, maybe it's both!"

Approaching the checkpoint booth, Rachel rolled down the passenger side window of the Camry, passing her driver's license to the stationed deputy. Staring at the item with close scrutiny, he took a brief look at her before passing the license back. He then waved for her to move forward. Rolling the window back up, she shifted the car out of neutral and into drive, taking it ahead to the parking lot. She had arrived about a half an hour before the usual visitor admittance time, so she had no problem finding a parking spot.

Getting out of the car right away, she caught glimpse of four other young women who were also waiting for the visitor doors to open. Rachel could hear the group gossiping about their boyfriends as she walked over to where the group stood by the doors. Before she knew it, she found herself joining into the conversation and talking about Blaze. She was filled with happiness and joy as she spoke about their relationship. There was no fronting either, because she truly spoke from her heart.

The young ladies were in mid-conversation when a female correctional officer walked out of the visitor door entrance. With a smile she stated, "OK, ladies you can come in now." By this time, about thirteen other visitors were waiting.

Inside the visiting room, the visitors were directed to stand in line because they had to be signed into a visitor's logbook. Rachel was the third one in line, and when it was her turn, the officer asked her, "What's your name?"

"Rachel Madison"

"Sign your name here," the officer stated as he pointed at the small space on the lined sheet of paper in the logbook. Once she completed this, he asked, "Who are you here to see?"

"Jermaine Johnson," she stated smiling. Just saying his name caused her blood pressure to rise. Looking at the officer as he keyed everything into the computer, she hoped that it would not take long to be processed.

After typing all the needed information into the computer the officer looked up at her saying. "Okay, Ms. Madison, it'll be about ten minutes."

That's all she needed to hear, so she walked back to the waiting area. As she sat impatiently, she watched the surrounding area with curiosity. She noticed right away that the majority of the visitors were female. Some were mothers and family members, while most of them were girlfriends and wives of the men they came to see.

Blaze was in the shower when the officer on the tier screamed out, "Johnson, on the visit."

"I'm in the shower, I'll be right out." He screamed as he rushed to rinse the soap off his body. This took less than thirty seconds, and then it took about another minute for him to dry off and put some boxers on. Walking back to his cell with a pair of shower clogs and a towel around his neck he shivered as the cold air hit his damp skin. He was fully dressed and ready to go, three minutes later.

Before leaving his cell to go on the visit, Blaze grabbed one of Rachel's pictures from off the shelf and it looked at it deeply for a few seconds. Then he kissed the picture, leaving a full lip imprint due to the moisture from his face.

"Where are you going, on a visit?" One of the cats on the gallery asked as Blaze high-stepped past him.

Without turning around he answered, "Yeah, my boo is probably down there." He knew for a fact that Rachel was the one visiting him because he basically had no on else besides his team behind him. His mother did not want anything to do with him anymore. She told him that if he could not abide by her rules, then he had to leave. And that's exactly how it had been since that day. He didn't even bother to call her to let her know that he was locked up.

"Johnson?" the C.O. asked him.

"Yeah," Blaze replied as he inched forward to the swinging gate, waiting for the officer to open it. Once the C.O. let him through, the officer was supposed to pat frisk him; but instead, he told Blaze to go ahead to the lobby.

Entering the lobby a C.O. and a sergeant sat behind a desk chatting. Seeing Blaze the C.O. asked, "What's your name?"

"Jermaine Johnson," Blaze replied as he walked over to the holding pen near the elevator shaft. After standing there for a moment listening to the two officer's conversation, the elevator, reaching the floor, came to life as the doors slipped open. An officer inside the elevator told Blaze to get in.

"Where are you going?" the officer asked, standing in front with his back facing Blaze.

"Visit" was his reply.

The elevator hit ground floor in a matter of seconds. And once the door opened, the officer told Blaze to go on to the visiting area, which was down the hallway.

Coming into the visiting room entrance, Blaze had to wait behind five other prisoners who had to be pat-frisked. One by one, they went through the ritual, spreading their legs and then placing their hands against the wall. Walking into the visiting area, Blaze made a right and walked over to give the officer on duty his name.

After looking down at the logbook for a moment, the C.O. directed Blaze to table twenty-three. Knowing the visiting area well enough Blaze knew that twenty-three had to be in the second row. No visitors were present in the area because they were usually called in after the first group of prisoners was called down to begin the visiting session. So for about five minutes, Blaze sat basically looking at the four walls around him, and then back and fourth at the outside visitor gates which is where visitors entered the visiting room after going through a metal detector.

The gate opened and he could see his baby girl standing among the other ladies looking delicious. She was wearing a pair of high-heeled leather boots, which came up about nine inches from the heel, a pair of blue jeans and some type of laced silk black shirt. The look was sporty, yet classy at the same time and he loved every bit of it.

Approaching the officers' station, she immediately noticed him staring at her. A smile lit her face as they took notice of one another. She didn't hear the officer say "Number twenty-three." Instead, she was caught up, striding toward the love of her life. Coming eye to eye with one another, they immediately embraced and shared a tongue kiss that lasted for about two minutes. Everyone in the visiting room, including the two officers, watched the two expressing their love for one another. Once they both let go, they sat staring at one another for a couple of seconds before either of them could catch their breath and say anything.

"How's my baby been doing?" he asked her smiling.

"Well, you know I could be doing better. But someone that we both know cannot stay out of trouble."

"Who could that be?" he asked, pretending to be confused.

"You, you little jerk" she stated laughing, and then went on "I should smack you for being such a bad ass. What did the lawyer say anyway?"

Looking down at the table in front of them he stopped smiling at once, "Man, this guy says they want to give me a four to life. As a matter of fact, I have to call him at three. I---" He stopped in mid-sentence and let his eyes wander around the room. Rachel's face was blank of all emotion and any signs that would let him know what she was thinking. He began to wish that he did not tell her the truth. All she did was watch him, looking into his eyes and then at his face. But she didn't say a word.

For what seemed to be ten minutes, but was instead no more than ten seconds, the two sat and just looked at one another, communicating silently. Blaze wanted answers, so therefore, he decided to break the ice.

"So what are you going to do if I have to do four years?"

"Are you going to do the whole four years?" she asked with sincere curiosity.

"Well, I can get work release after two, you know like Ronda's boyfriend does.

Smiling mischievously she looked at him shyly, "Am I gonna be your wife? I think that would help, don't you?"

Blaze did not know what to say, and he almost choked on his saliva while trying to think of the right words to reply. Nevertheless, he managed.

"Rachel, it's all up to you. You already know that I love you, and that I'm not trying to lose you. So if this is what you want to do, let's do this."

She smiled at his reply and began giggling hysterically, holding her hands to her face as she looked at him. For the next twenty minutes, they talked about everything without even mentioning the subject of marriage once again.

As the visiting session was coming to a close, the visiting room officer walked around with his clipboard, telling everyone in the first group that their visit was over. Seeing the officer coming their way, Blaze decided to do what he had to do before the officer came so they could have a little more time. Standing up, Blaze grabbed both of Rachel's shoulders, pulling her up on her feet as he began to tongue kiss her passionately. Letting go of her, he stroked the back of her head asking, "Are you going to be OK?"

"Yeah, I think I will be all right" she replied, before putting her right hand to her mouth saying "Oh! Jasheem's girlfriend called me, and she said that they have him in Nassau and that their going to bring him over here after he takes care of a case over there."

"Oh, word!" Blaze replied, before Rachel cut him off.

"And I hope that when you come home you leave that Brotherhood shit alone and go to school. We have enough money, and I'll make sure you're good when you come home.

Blaze did not reply because although Rachel was staring at him with darted eyes, she also had a smile mixed with a smirk. Then, as if she forgot something really important, she stated before walking off blowing him a kiss, "Oh! And your moms said to call her after she gets home. She wants to speak to you, she's worried, since when you came home the last time and did not stop by to see here. She thinks you hate her. And she said to call your dad as soon as you get off the visit with me because, he's worried too." She looked at Blaze smirking, at the same time shaking her head side to side.

Blaze did not know whether to be angry or happy with her. And she did not wait for him to say anything before turning on her heels and walking to the front. He hadn't spoken to his mother in the last five or six months. She gave him an ultimatum to change or to leave. Once gone, he knew she could never accept the person that he had evolved into. The street life had turned him into her worst nightmare. His dad, Trini was another story. He didn't want anything to do with the man, but he was not going to hold a grudge against him for the rest of his life. He was a man now making decisions for himself.

Walking away from the visiting room Blaze thought to himself, "I need a change, maybe I will go to school after all. I'll do it for me and Infinite." Flashbacks of the past and all the events that lead to him being the person that he was, now played in slow motion. His heart skipped a beat as he thought about Infinite and how when they were little kids, they were the best of friends and had the most terrific mothers in the world. Once Infinite went to prison that first time, everything changed. Infinite changed and from there, Blaze had changed too. "Man, I miss you!" Blaze whispered, balling his left hand into a fist while he palmed it with the right. Aimlessly, he walked back to his house unit.

Epilogue

Time stops for no one, even though Blaze, Jasheem and Papo were out of the game, the game did not stop. Within a day or two, there were others willing to risk it all for the love of money.

As Blaze walked back to his cell, Detective Aldoe and Detective Jackson stood side by side in Captain Kozak's office getting verbally assaulted as usual.

Ms. Simmons, the reporter, sat behind her desk going over some case she was working on.

When Freedom disappeared to go on the run, he left a half-kilo at the spot, so now Jah-Jah, Shawn, Ray-Ray, and Mike were the key members of MPR. A forest green Cherokee Limited Edition jeep sat outside at the curb in front of Mama's apartment as the four of them sat with her eating one of her famous home cooked meals.

Freedom was on a greyhound bus, and was headed to Montgomery, Alabama with a kilo and thirty thousand in a duffle bag placed on top of the rack directly over one of the seats in the back of the bus. He sat near the middle, and every now and then he'd steal a peak to make sure the bag was still there.

Born didn't have a trouble in the world, he got out the trouble he was in by setting his childhood friend up. And as Jasheem sat in jail watching MTV rap videos, Born, on the other hand, was sleeping comfortably.

Dictionary

Beast: Police, law enforcement

Cipher: Person place or thing. Or an imaginary square that one stands upon to represent truth and justice.

Doe: Money

Five Percenter: A splinter group, which evolved from the Nation of Islam. Their philosophy is that the creator is Lord of all the worlds, and that Man is god of his own mind, body and spirituality.

Gee: Homeboy, friend

Glock: Semi-automatic weapon "gun"

god: A Five Percenter term referring to man possessing knowledge of himself. Man "mind."

Hustler: Someone who is proactive in going after and obtaining money.

Kilo: 1,000 grams

Pistol-whip: To smack someone with a gun.

Steel: Gun

Sun: Another term used to define friend. A Five Percenter Term. Symbolism, in representation of man being the center of his universe like the sun.

Don't miss out on *Survivor*, Therone Shellman's autobiography scheduled to be released in the fall of 2007. Keep reading to get a taste of what's to come.

Survivor

The autobiography
of
Therone Shellman

Excerpt from Book One

I would get up early every Saturday and Sunday go to the store to buy either a quart of milk or sixteen ounces of orange juice before going on my mission to catch the fiends (crack addicts) making their rounds through the hood from five thirty to seven thirty AM. Usually I'd make anywhere from $100 to $350 just between these hours. And then I'd go to the spot somewhere between eight and ten AM.

On my way back from the store one day I noticed a light blue Celebrity, which kept circling around the two blocks I had just passed. I figured the driver noticed me as well. I never served the guy, but I had seen him through the hood copping from some of the dealers who played the corners on the other side of town. I was on a mountain bike because it was not safe to drive through the hood. Plus, it was only a thirteen block radius, so I either stayed on foot or on bicycle just in case I needed to get away from the police by cutting through some house or dodging through a wooded path.

As the car made its way toward my direction, I turned and surveyed the area to make sure five-o (police) was not around, and then I flagged the driver down. Once he approached I could see that he was the same cat I'd seen around before.

"Yo! What up?" I asked. I did not want to say any numbers or talk about money just in case he was trying to set someone up for a buy and bust or sale.

He was a scrawny white guy who looked like he had been on the shit for some time. There were dark spots around his eyes, and his face was sucked in, hair disheveled, shirt was wrinkled. And there was an odor that only a dealer or someone who had been around crack cocaine smokers could detect. It was a stale, smoky smell that was a lot different than cigarette smoke.

"Do you have a hundred?" he asked, fidgeting before interjecting, " It's real, right? Can I try it? I don't want to get beat." He had a cracked front tooth and white stuff on his lips, which looked like foam. I did not want him to spit on me so I kept my distance.

I was annoyed and never in the mood to make small talk with any of them, so I told him I was about business.

"I see you all the time on the block fucking with them cats who come to us. I don't fuck around. And I do not have no time for bullshit. Go around the block and come back. I got them CDs for you, so take your shit and get the fuck outta here. That's the way it is, and that's the only way it's going down!"

He realized right away even through his crack high that I was not bullshitting, and I was not out to beat anyone, and I really did not have or want to make the time to have a conversation with him.

"OK, OK, I got you. I think I seen you around. Give me your number. I—"

I did not say anything, but instead cut his words short with my stare, which told the story of what was going on in my mind.

"You're wearing my patience thin. Didn't I tell you what to do? Let's conduct business so we can both go about our business."

Without speaking he stepped on the gas and disappeared around the block. I was in front of my friend's house, so I took the bike and placed it on the side of the fence. Walking to a tree, I took out a half-gram package from the Ziploc bag, which had about ten other packages inside, and then I buried the Ziploc bag in a shallow grave. I stood up in the cut by the tree so that I could scan both sides of the block. I always was on the lookout for police, no matter where I was in the hood because I was on parole and had just finished doing four and a half years. I still had seven and a half years of parole.

I saw the Celebrity as it screeched around the corner. I still stayed close to the tree to make sure another car was not following behind. As the car approached to within a few yards from where I stood, I stepped out to the side of the street.

Grabbing the Ben Franklin, I looked it over quickly, scanned the streets one more time, and then gave the white man the package along with a slip of paper, which held my pager number. I kept no less than five slips of paper in my pocket at any given time because I sold to drugs dealers as well as users.

Seeing the package brought a glow and smile to his face. He looked down at the package in his hand and then up at me.

"This is way more than what I get. I'm a call you," he stuttered and then continued, "'cause I have a lot of friends who buy! I'm a…"

I did not stand around so that he could continue babbling. I walked across the street over to the bike while he sped off. Once he was out of sight, I looked around again to make sure all was good. Feeling satisfied, I ran quickly to the stash, dug it up, put it in one of my army pants pockets and ran back to the bike. I was thirsty so I pulled the quart of milk out of the bag and began guzzling it down. I was used to drinking a quart of milk at least four days a week, so I drank it in five minutes. Feeling good, I stretched out, yawned, and walked over to the garbage can, throwing the bag and empty container in it.

Looking at my watch, I realized that I needed to make rounds quickly before the other dealers came out. Getting up early on the weekends helped me add at least one new customer to my pager a week. While the other cats played the blocks, I got my money through calls and from customers who came to our spot, as well as a few corner dealers to whom I would front packages. Once they were done, I would get my money and give them another package. With this system I was always making money, no matter whether I was around or not.

That morning was pretty good. As soon as I got on my bike again I caught one of my regulars coming down the block. She was only good for twenty dollars at a time, but she only spent her money with me, so she was good for two hundred dollars each week. After her I caught about three to four other customers and decided to take it in to rest up a bit before I started the day up at the spot.

The Spot

On the weekends I opened up because my partner would not come until sometime between eleven AM and noon. He opened up during the week and stayed until I would come around five PM from school. I was going to school for barbering because I wanted to open up a barbershop/salon.

After bagging up an ounce in half-gram packages, and weighing a half ounce and then two ounces I bagged everything up separately. I then went to my bottom dresser drawer and grabbed a .38 snub nose and jetted out to the spot. Once there I went to the door to let Harry know that I was there, so he could open the side door and I could set up. Harry lived in the house and let us sell out of it as long as we fed him with base every day. As soon as I greeted him, I gave him a bump, a quick wake up piece.

Within a few minutes I was set up. I had the scale, a few baggies, and two rigged cell phones in the room, which had a door which opened to the outside of the house. After setting up I quickly got out of there. Harry had a dog, a mutt who was infested with fleas, ticks, and whatever else. He let the dog roam through the whole house, so I was scared that something would jump in my hair. I had dreadlocks, which were down to my shoulders, and the last thing I wanted was for a tick or flea to find a home in them. I did not like being in Harry's side of the house either because from the looks of him he seemed no better off than the dog. The house was filthy and the floors and the walls were dingy. There was always a sense of moisture in the air, and even if the lights were on, it always seemed dark. Harry took showers every day, I suppose, and did not smell, but his clothes were always dingy, hair disheveled, and his pale skin had a gray tone to it. The man gave me the creeps. Not that I was scared of him as if he intimidated me. Instead he gave me the creeps the same way that a character from a spooky movie would give someone the creeps. He was very smart, and was always working on radios and electronic gadgets, fixing them up. At one time he had a very high paying job and lived very well. But his wife divorced him, and I guess that was when he turned to drugs.

Standing outside I surveyed my surroundings. I rarely ever sat down at the spot because it was situated in from the street and I could not see both angles of cars coming unless I stood in the driveway or in front of the house. I learned in prison to always be aware of who and what was around me at all times, so I never slept on my feet.

At the end of the gate I saw Bee come out of his house and start walking in my direction. As he got to me he smiled.

"Damn!" he said. "You're a true hustler. You be up bright and early in the morning like clockwork." We gave each other a pound.

"I got that for you right now," I told him.

"Where's this guy?" he asked as we walked up the driveway.

"He'll probably be here in an hour or so. You know he be out tricking late at night."

We both started laughing. I went inside, came out a few seconds later, and handed him the package.

"This is a half?" he asked.

"Yeah! Give me four hundred."

Bee sat down in one of the chairs out front. I stood all the time as we talked with the package of drugs in my left front pocket and the .38 in the right.

"I can't believe he got out that quick," Bee said.

"Yeah. I don't know about this because I asked his wife what happened, and she ain't saying nothing. She came by here Thursday with his slut ass sister. She called me to the car trying to talk to me. But I ain't fucking with her. She be fucking all these lames around here and then got the nerve to think I'd fuck with her." Pausing to think for a second, I then continued. "But back to him, all I know is that he been acting funny the last two weeks. He makes crazy money, but he don't know how to manage it. I think he's getting mad that his customers are starting to fuck with me more than him. Even the connect shows me more love than him. You know all I do is save. That flashy shit will get a nigga knocked."

"I don't know, V," Bee said, "but shit seems kind of fishy. Yeah, I don't think he likes the fact that ever since he brought you over here you been doing your thing. Now he gets from you. It's like it's your spot now because everyone comes to see you. Niggas don't have no respect for him. That's why he has you over here. He knows niggas ain't gonna fuck with him when you're around. They used to just take shit and keep it moving. He likes you, but at the same time I think he got animosity toward you. He's pussy. Everyone knows it and so does he. He aint gonna…"

A customer showed up, so Bee stopped talking and let me serve him. Then a few of Bee's cousins showed up. Within ten minutes there were about six people, including me, conversing in front of the spot. They all were sitting down talking. I still stood, and in fact walked to the end of the driveway so that I could see both street entrances.

EJ, my partner in the spot, showed up, getting dropped off by a customer. We shook hands and I let him know that all was good and where the two ounces were. He looked tired and had a look on his face as if he was seriously contemplating something. Without exchanging many words he walked into the spot. No more than five to seven minutes later George, the same customer who dropped him off, pulled up alongside the entrance of the driveway.

"I'll be back. I have to use the phone!" I heard EJ say to the crowd as he passed them. Once he reached me, he said, "I have to go use the phone. Do you want anything from the store?"

"Get me an orange juice," I told him.

They pulled off and came back ten minutes later. By this time I was no longer standing by the entrance of the driveway. Instead I was in conversation with Bee. I told him to take the drugs I gave him and to put the package up. He agreed and laughed, realizing that sitting there with a package in his pocket doing nothing was kind of dumb. We shook hands and agreed to get up later. He walked down the block home.

I was on edge and I didn't know why. I took my orange juice that EJ bought and began drinking it. I was not paying any attention to the guys who were there. They were shooting dice and talking with EJ, who was a big gambler.

All I heard was, "Five-O is coming! They are everywhere!"

Immediately I dropped the orange juice, looked up, and saw Slick and Dane come down the street on bicycles. They were screaming "Five-O" at the top of their lungs. I said nothing and began running toward the backyard. Some of the other guys had started before me, but I caught up, pushing them out the way. I could hear cars pulling up to the front of the house, tires screeching, doors slamming, and people yelling.

I did not have time to think for one split second. I just relied on instinct. As I reached the backyard I jumped over the fence of the next house, just barely using my hands to lift me. Once in the yard I dodged trees, running to the front of the house. Once on the street I could see detectives and guys wearing task force jackets everywhere. I ran past one, but he grabbed one of the guys who was running next to me, and I was able to just breeze by him.

Miraculously, I reached the next block and ran into the woods situated next to a fenced-in house. There were two young girls, about fourteen to fifteen years old, sitting on the house stoop, and they saw me dodge into the woods. They did not scream or say anything. In fact, they acted normal. And they did not tell police who questioned them that they saw someone run into the woods. I could hear the conversation. I swore to myself that I was going to buy them whatever they wanted if I did not get caught.

Once inside the woods I weighed my options quickly. I could keep running or seek refuge there until I saw someone pass by the next block, and then get a ride out of there. I decided to stay because on the next block there was a church, which had about a half acre of open land for me to pass through before I would reach houses or areas to hide. Comfortable with this decision, I quickly buried my gun and the drugs near a tree that was easy to remember.

I calmed myself and stood close to a tree, seeking to camouflage myself. I was wearing a fatigued sleeveless vest and fatigue pants along with black Travel Fox sneakers, so I blended in well with the surroundings.

Going back to jail is not an option, I thought and then I saw a familiar car coming toward the next block. It was Razor. Looking around toward both blocks I saw it was clear so I ran out of the woods into the backyard of the house and toward the front. Luckily he saw me and began to slow down.

"I'll give you one hundred dollars. Just get me out of here."

"Get in."

I got in on the passengers side and lay along the backseat.

"Take me home. Get me the fuck out of here."

"What happened? They have both blocks blocked off. They're even checking serial numbers on bicycles."

He kept rambling on, but got quiet when I told him my thoughts.

"I think EJ tried to set me up. He left to use the phone when we have two phones in the house. He knows this already."

Look for other upcoming titles to be
released by Third Eye Publishing in
the fall of 2007.

**Third Eye Publishing is a company where knowledge
reigns supreme. Please visit our Web site for author
submission guidelines.**

www.thirdeyepublishing.org
www.myspace.com/thirdeyepublishing